D1287534

In Full Possession

HELEN FLINT

In Full Possession

St. Martin's Press
New York

Library of Congress Cataloging-in-Publication Data

Flint, Helen.
      In full possession / Helen Flint.
          p.   cm.
     ISBN 0-312-03848-8
     I. Title.
  PR6056.L53I6   1989   89-27045
  823'.914—dc20   CIP

First published in Great Britain by William Heinemann Ltd.

10 9 8 7 6 5 4 3 2

To all my Johns, especially J.C.,
to redress the balance?

Acknowledgements

I would like to thank Paul Burgess
for legal advice concerning the plot.
Also all those who looked after my
children so that I could write.

Part One

Part 3

1 *Homecoming*

Until this afternoon Bet had looked forward to a ripe old senility, to playing hide-and-seek with words and memories in a mist of pleasant confusion. Instead, she now sits in her high-backed chair, the last traces of a rose pattern just leaving it, in the dingy back room, waiting for Benedict, in full and perfect possession of all her faculties, her memories astonishingly bright and accurate: with each bat of the eyelid a decade unfolds.

On her lap is an avalanche of multicoloured acrylic wool and in her right hand, the knuckles a little swollen, a little reddened, a crochet hook leans along which the slight tremor of the hand is conducted, magnified.

It is the same tremor, the same pain, and she knows now that she will not last the winter, perhaps not the month.

It is not death she fears, not now, but it is leaving Benedict on his own, preparing him for solitude. Now she will have to do it, since there is to be no pre-medication for this final operation, she will go into it cold.

Hearing his bicycle against the broken gate, his footsteps on the stone at the front, his key in the door, she frames herself to play the game for him, and to play it well. The room holds its breath.

His presence out in the hall and the sound of his work-weary voice.

'You dead yet, Mother?'

'That you, Benny?'

'No, madam, Boston Strangler.'

'Come on in, Boston.' Her melodic old voice with a twang of Yorkshire, gentrified ever so slightly (it will wear off as tiredness overtakes her this evening), undulates down the hallway as he turns and shuts the door, kicking Geoffrey, the stuffed dachshund, against the draught.

One look at the room and he attacks her, hands around the neck.

'I shall have to take your miserable little life, Mrs Ashe, because

3

you have disobeyed me and not put on the gas fire when it is two below zero outside!'

Her neck like folds of old satin over pipe cleaners. He kisses her smiling face, on the powdery petal of cheek. Everything to him, the whole world, and she risks hypowhatsits.

'Save me the trouble of dying,' she says, kneading the mound of coloured wools as Ben bends to light the cracked ceramic of the hissing fire.

'This is something we call winter, Mother. Or have you forgotten?'

'It's like burning five pound notes.'

'How is our blanket, Mother? They are waiting in Africa for that very thing. Make it big enough for the whole lot of them to snuggle under together.'

She says nothing. The fire has caught. Ben glances only at her face.

'What's up, doc?' He bares his front teeth at her, still kneeling. She makes to get out of the chair.

'I'll put kettle on.'

'Stay where you are!' he says, growling.

'I am expert at that,' under her breathy bosom, heaving back into the stuffing of a thousand undustings. A cloud of damp motes rises, and falls back onto the grubby white of her gathered blouse. Ben has not noticed the tremor. If he had, he would have mentioned the imaginary four bottles of gin she had imbibed. For each and every disaster, Ben has a joke. A comfort, such a comfort to me. I shall miss him when I'm gone. No that's not quite right.

Leaving the room Ben switches on the television absent-mindedly, as if it were a light. Children's *Newsround* issues into the room.

In Africa the monsoon has failed and they are in desperate need of an acrylic, multicoloured, crocheted blanket big enough to insulate the entire continent. There is a rumour that such a thing is being made at this very moment in Sheffield.

At least it was until this afternoon.

Many sorts of (geriatric) humour are available to Ben these days, but being the endearingly helpless male unable to cope in his own kitchen (a favourite on the box) is not one of them. If

4

kitchen it can be called. Designed as the prison for a Victorian skivvy, it has changed little. The sink is still white, cracked porcelain, the bowls are still white enamel with a thin blue stripe, the hand-held tin opener the only modern convenience. The walls and ceilings were once painted white gloss to be hygienic and are now peeling beige. Benny wipes a porthole in the grey window and looks out.

Summer and winter alike it is dark along Psalter Lane. True, in high summer, as high as Sheffield ever is, a green haze just filters through the bright green canopy of broad lime leaves a hundred feet above the road; so that those walking to town struggle to breathe and see, as if underwater in a fishtank which needs a good swilling out.

Sticky-roofed, leaking and in much need of repair, once grand Victoriana bristles along the avenue. Four- and five-storey houses, rooms to let, bedsittered, benefits houses. Barely a family left.

But Ben is on the other side of the house, the north side, and he only sees the narrow alley between his kichen and Mrs Harrison's – which is also not a family home, for she takes in Distressed Gentlemen (white only) on the Assistance. Barely a real family left.

'Cept me and Mother, thinks Benedict, swinging the string-wound metal handle of the kettle from the gas ring to the waiting globe of the teapot. The tea-bag spins clockwise. Down under, Sharon's spins the other way. And her tea is iced. 'Cept me and Mother. And the Lodger.

For even Benny and his mother are not truly just a family: they have an Upper Tenant. Unfurnished flat on the top floor. Where She lives. She they never speak with, Her.

Mother's tea in the one china cup (nothing is too good for you) and his in the blue and white striped mug. Can you bear to miss *Blue Peter*? Just this once. How to remove the cup from its saucer without giving it all away, without a clatter? He turns down the sound from a remote control device on the mantelpiece.

'The whole point of this is to have it in your lap, Mother, not somewhere else. Not out of reach.'

'The television has fallen off.'

'The *programmes* I hope you mean.'

'Oh, stop – I'll spill it.'

Benny sits on the arm of her armchair where she cannot see his face. Abruptly tiredness swoops down over his face headlong like the negative of rapid beams of car headlights unexpectedly flashing over an indoor wall in the twilight. This rapid shadow, grey on the unnatural suntan, a jaundice, of his high cheekbones. He looks, in a flash, all of forty. Bet doesn't see, though she knows. If only, if only she could float into confusion, now and tomorrow and for ever.

'I suppose Lady Muck came down for a little chat this afternoon?'

Bet manages a smile for him. 'No, but only because she was at work, I'm sure.'

'That's the trouble with this country, Mother, too much employment. Ruining the art of little chats.'

'As if she would, Ben!'

For tea Benny offered her, tea-towel draped over his arm, the choice between beans on toast with poached egg, spaghetti hoops on toast, with poached egg, or macaroni cheese. It was his custom to give her the illusion of choosing. This afternoon, suddenly annoyed with the twitching 'Italian' eyebrows, she declared she was spoilt for choice and would have the steak with chips.

Every night they had steak and chips; something resembling poached egg, and never in the slightest reminding them of Sharon's barbecued meals in Australia.

Over tea, taken on lap-trays before the muted children's pro-grammes on the television, Bet asked if there was any News (sometimes Benny felt as if he were her foreign correspondent in the outer world – dispatches from an unspecified front), so he related, quite deadpan, so that she would not believe a word of it, how twenty stolen television sets had come into the workshop, all with the same mysterious fault, which he had righted, and then had all disappeared. And how he had borrowed the van to visit an old dear who wanted Ceefax installed, and found, when

6

he got to her house, that the set was an original 1954 model. It didn't even receive ITV.

'Benny, you could have been something,' she said, the crumbly bits of a Mr Kipling's Fairy Cake wandering down her smockfront.

'Pardon me, I am something.'

'But anything. You were so bright at school and . . . it's never too late.'

'Ah, you mean Prime Minister.'

'Seriously, Ben.'

Benny took her plate and made for the door to the kitchen. 'I'll try harder to be Mrs Thatcher, Mother, if that's what you want. But it's not going to be easy. For one thing, I'm too young, and for another, there's no downstairs toilet at No. 10 I know for a fact, and that wouldn't suit you, would it?'

'You could install one, dear.' What will he have left when I go? What will he do?

Ben's father, so he had been told over and over again, had risen up through the Water Board, like a cork.

The future Prime Minister washed up the dishes, in the ceramic square sink under the non-transparent window (so next-door can't see thee in thy apron).

One day soon, a few more thousand televisions under his belt, so to speak, he will modernise this dump. You won't recognise it, Mother. I hope I will recognise my own kitchen where I bathed you and Sharon a few decades ago. Bat, bat, flip of the eyelid – just a few decades. As if yesterday lay in wait beyond tomorrow.

It is only six o'clock now. He will aim to have Bet in bed by nine, packed in with hotties like a reversed salmon in ice. When they return.

Ben rejoins his Mother and elaborately reminds her it is the evening of the Over-16s, or is it 60s, dance tonight at the church hall. She confesses she is not up to it. Fine, then she won't mind if he takes up one of the fifty-three offers from Buxom Young Wenches for an evening of torrid passion. No, dear, you go. He didn't think he was up to it either. Walk the dog then, Geoffrey hasn't been out all week.

Ben puts on his donkey jacket, checks the cash in his pocket, kisses her on the soft, furry, grey crown of her head (suddenly, alarmingly, he notices how much skull-skin he can now see between the sparse hairs), and unbolts the front door, bending to take Geoffrey's lead, a length of string, in the left hand. This he threads under the door as he leaves, so that Geoffrey is taut against the draught once more.

He tiptoes round the house, down the alley between his house and Mrs Harrison and quietly enters by the back door. He intends, as he often does when supposedly at the pub, to sit in the kitchen and read the newspaper for half an hour. Bet is slightly confused these days, though she denies it strenuously, and *thinks* hours have gone by. Instead he sits but leaves the newspaper folded where it lies, amidst the debris on the formica table, thinking. Something is wrong with Bet, but he doesn't know what. He has noticed a tremor.

The door to Bet's room is opening, slowly. Ben can hear the television, music and canned laughter. She drifts into the hall, trembling, catches sight of a man sitting in the kitchen at the table and screams. Ben runs to her and catches her before she hits the ground.

'I changed my mind, that's all. Don't be . . . it's only me!'

'I thought, I thought . . .,' said Bet.

Ben escorted her to the downstairs toilet and back to her chair.

Bet is sitting in her chair, nothing is really different – she still fills every bit of it with her amplitude, but her skin is the colour of mushroom, her cheeks wet with tears, smiling at him. He can see that the Old Trouble has taken her again.

'Why didn't you tell me?'

In disaster, during those moments when the real world staggers and shifts about us and unspeakable danger seems seconds away, many of us promise God the earth (you can have it back now!), in return for this one favour, this one measly – couldn't you, God, just this once, spare the axe?

But Ben – anarchist and iconoclast by nature – promises Bet everything. He will not leave her alone for more than one minute, he will do up the house around her, it will be a palace, so hot the plants (the ones he will install along with the pine panelling) will die off. He will make the lodger pay more and they will live like kings, have everything delivered to the house. He will have a jacuzzi installed for her, if she would just, please, can you move at all, Mother? No? Never mind, the doctor is here, I can hear his car.

As he encircled her great solid shoulders with his arm, he was put in mind of a garden statue of a fawn which as a child he mistook for real and bent to stroke. The soft strands of fur were hard and gritty. The spasm of Bet's muscles resembled stone itself.

'Well,' said the doctor, afterwards, helpfully, 'every day is another day.'
    'Sorry?'
    'I mean, we must be grateful, after all your mother has not had a stroke, which is not uncommon at her age, and she has just had a marvellous holiday in Australia and she says she can return there whenever she likes.'
    'Well, strictly speaking . . .'
    'Look, do whatever you can to go back there. This cold and damp — I'd give her a few weeks at most. She says she was *swimming* in the sea over there just a month ago. Is that true?'
    Benedict smiled. 'Yes, like a woman of thirty.'
    'Then send her back to your sister. It'll prolong her life.'
    'I can't. My sister sent the money, you see . . .'
    'Ah, come on, these houses are worth a fair bit now I hear. Sell up and move out there. Better life all round. Wish I could go myself.'
    Benedict, who hourly joked of death with Bet, could hardly bring himself to ask.
    'How long has she got?'
    'I can't say that. Three weeks or three years. There's no saying. Elderly people can just give up sometimes. Even while a loving son is caring for them. Witness her rejuvenation in Australia. How do you account for that?'
    'The weather?'
    'Rubbish. The sun visits us now and then. It's more than that. It's a state of mind.'
    'You mean dying is a state of mind?' asked Benedict, genuinely

9

astonished to hear a medical man, to him a priest of science, saying this, expressing this mystical uncertainty. As if he had dared to say to a customer, it might work for a few weeks, I can't say, try giving it a good kick.

'Haven't you known elderly couples who die, of natural causes, within days of each other?'

'Yes.'

'Well then.'

Benedict stood on the top step by the front door, watching the doctor wade through the fallen leaves to his car in the dark evening.

Ben wanted to say, but could not find the words, that those people were alone, had nothing to live for; and his mother had him, and, therefore, everything to live for.

The doctor pulled his camel-hair coat about him, and drove away.

Her Triumph TR7 slid into the slot left by the doctor under the lime tree, and she herself, Margueritte, slipped silkily out from the driver's seat and, briefcase in one hand and a pile of exercise books in the other, pushing the navy blue door shut with her hip, came up the steps towards Benedict.

'Mother's poorly,' he said, without looking at her, 'doctor's just been.'

'Oh really? I am sorry to hear that,' she said in her flat tones, her foreign, southern voice, like some posh nobody on the radio.

You are not, liar, you are not at all sorry.

Benedict followed her in and watched her swish and sway up the stairs over her stilettos, making no dent in the threadbare carpet of the hall stairs.

He went in to Mother, now in her bed, dozing, tranquillised.

Tidying the room and slotting in hotties, he told her, under his breath, that there was nothing wrong with her, she was a malingerer, it had got to stop. The doctor had prescribed a short run before breakfast followed by a cold bath, and that he had decided they would sell the house and move to Australia permanently.

*

Bet may have heard him, on the periphery of her anaesthetised consciousness. Who knows? Somehow the next morning she seemed to remember what was to come. The good man's medication was doing the work nature would not – it was clouding her mind wonderfully. And this may have been the pre-knowledge of senility: a perception born of temporal confusion. When tomorrow is so like yesterday, which do you anticipate, which remember? Only the long, long past is really clearly, vividly fixed.

He undressed upstairs in his own room, and slept in a sleeping-bag on the floor next to Bet, listening to the quiet breathing of her drugged sleep.

The next morning he made two phone calls, one to the workshop explaining that he would not be coming in until further notice. Charlie took the call himself and offered to send round the Mrs, which sounded more like a threat than an offer of help. Unemployment was not something Ben feared, for the more Sheffield fell into a workless condition, the more people sat in front of their sets, and the more imperative it became to have them mended within the hour.

The second call was to an estate agent whose offices lay on his route to work.

Waiting for the estate agent, having rallied Bet into her chair, washed and polished and radio earphones on, Benedict went into the back garden, where old machinery and television carcasses vied with rose and blackberry bushes for an inch of light.

It was not so much that nature was reclaiming Ben's garden, for it had never been colonised in the first place – it was more a question of the imperialism of technology. There is, for example, near the back door by the outside toilet, a rockery of television carcasses with shy Alpine batteries and hollow, wandering valve-wires creeping between the protruding brown melamine corners of underground boxes. Furry, frayed, three-core cable winds round the stems of three-legged television stands, planted in remembrance of chrome splendour in the days when Bet rented out six rooms, all with sets on meters. The meters themselves are

11

dormant at the far end among nature's only ambassador – the blackberry. Under the thin, spurred shadow of dusty barbed wire they huddle, their numbers meaning nothing, one of them with an old shilling planted ten years ago. One of Ben's clearest early memories was of his father planting coins on Christmas Eve. Ben assumed they would grow into a thrupenny tree, but apparently nobody had expected this, though neighbours were doing it too.

The rest is a tasteful display of bedding toasters, spring plugs, frames and shells of frames, all man-made, all vying with each other for the paler shades of darkness in this north-facing yard.

'My garden needs a woman's touch,' Ben once told a visiting friend, his employer.

'No, an Exocet missile would be better,' Charlie had replied. He had been in the Falklands. 'You could recycle this lot into a dump. Any bodies buried here?' Charlie thought always of violence and sudden death, though the outward signs of it were humorous. All his talk, all his codes. He sent Benny and the boys on missions, search and destroy. Yomp down the Ecclesall Road for me, Ben, and sort this out. Televisions were expiring, exploding, off-course, needed a good rodding, a seeing-to, last throes, kick up the bum. To Benny and the boys and Bet the Falklands war had happened on television, so it seemed only right that Charlie was now in command over a team who mended televisions.

Unaccustomed to being here and alone at this time of day, he stood, bemused, looking at the clouds overhead. Is living too just a state of mind?

'I see th'ave had doctor, then.'

Ben spun round. 'Oh, you noticed that did you?' He avoided the 'thee'. It was too friendly for the old goat.

Like one of those new duvets she overflowed over the edge of the wall, her soft white arms sighing feather-filled, settling into rolls over the mossy brickwork. Quiet as down too, she floated in and out of other people's lives. Her face, puffed and rough-red, chewed on itself with a sinister inexplicable movement, and she said, 'Only, if there's owt I can do, tha knows . . .'

'My mother could have done with a visit or two, Mrs Harrison. Not now, though, I'm staying with her.'

'Ah, I would 'ave visited but I've my gentlemen to see to,' she

12

said. She had two men and one couple on the Benefit. Hardly gentlemen. Well paid though. 'Is it a question of time, then, lad?'

Or, she means, can I now spread it about that Mrs Ashe is dying?

Ben approached the wall, aggressively. She did not move. 'We are none of us getting any younger, are we, Mrs Harrison?'

She was determined to get all the information she could. 'Only nowadays who can th'turn to? Neighbours either out all day, temporary, lodgers or', she bent nearer, nodding her head in the direction of his other neighbour, beyond the dying privet held together with cables and discarded flex, 'coloured.'

As Mrs Harrison informed a few people later in the Co-op, an estate agent came the same day, in the afternoon. Bet was up and walking with the aid of her two sticks and was determined to show him 'her floor' as she called it. She told him much about Australia, and Benedict was surprised at the interest he showed.

Benedict was not naïve, it was simply that he had enjoyed the good fortune not to have encountered, in all the thirty-eight years of his life, any estate agents. People who are born in, grow up in, and then continue to live in the same house, are so blessed.

Having seen the decayed remnants of the first floor of a grand Victorian family home, one which he even doubted had seen better times, ridiculously spacious living-room, equally capacious 'dining-room' where Bet slept, and several sculleries and coal holes all impersonating a kitchen, totally unmodernised, the agent suggested that he be shown the other floors.

Well, well, well, fancy this falling into his hands. Wondrous. No mod cons whatsoever. In nd. extens. modernisation. Scope DIY, family home or income, he dictated into his minute tape recorder. 3 floors. Tree-lined ave. Pop area nr schls and shops.

'Could the council lop these trees, do you think?' he asked breezily as Benedict led him up the stairs past a window entirely blocked by leaves.

'Why?'

'It's so dark here because of the trees. It might put potential buyers off a bit. Nothing to worry about though.' Benny showed

13

him the three bedrms, no rads, and bthrm, fittings *circa* 1949 and then stopped.

'And the attic floor. Inhabitable at all?' asked the agent, still breezy, still unaware.

'We have a flat up here,' said Benedict, starting the long narrow ascent to Her place, fumbling for the key. It was years since he had come up here.

'Ah, was the granny flat I s'pose?'

'No. There's a lodger.'

'Furnished, I hope.'

'No, it's all her furniture I believe.'

The agent stopped, mid-stair, one foot raised. As if he suspected the floor would give way under him.

'It's quite sound. I'll show you around.'

'You have a sitting tenant,' said the agent, putting his notepad and tiny tape-recorder back in his jacket pocket.

'It's all right,' said Benedict, 'it belongs to us, all of it.'

'But is he prepared to go?' asked the agent, looking out of the dark window.

'She'll have to, won't she?'

Is this man stupid or very clever? The agent subjected Benny to a valuation not unlike that which he used for property.

Circa 1948, or late thirties min, unmodernised mother's boy, single-storied, one-dimensional, rather thick, possibly cavity walls for brains, uninsulated against disaster by virtue of truncated education. In need tarting up for market, though not unattractive. No negs (not fat, not scarred, no visible tattoos from previous occupants) but few pos.

'You'll have to work at that one.'

'What d'you mean?'

'Use all the tactics you can. She has a right to stay, I think you'll find. Sometimes people settle out of court with a "consideration" which means money.'

'Who pays who?'

The agent laughed. 'You pay them. A couple of thousand usually. To go.'

'A couple of thousand! We haven't got any money at all.'

'Then you'll have to make it unpleasant for her to stay.'

'How?'

14

They started down the stairs – the agent evidently did not want to see around the flat, so Benny put the keys back in his pocket.

The agent, supposing that Benny was likely to understand him, spoke euphemistically of harassment, of loud music and poison letters, of large men drunk, threatening imaginary sitting tenants. Benedict listened, but did not take it in. Unlike Charlie's black statements, his illustrations of violence had no humorous gloss on them, and Benny was merely puzzled.

She would have to agree to leave. His mother would die soon if she did not return to Australia. The doctor had said so. There were no two ways about it. People in real life do the right thing, when it is clear what the right thing is. He would simply have to make it clear to her that the time had come for the end of her tenancy. That he required full possession of his own house, now.

'Will you come later to put up the For Sale sign, then?' he asked at the door.

'Well, look, son, when you've got her out, give me a ring. Until then there's nothing I can do. Houses with sitting tenants are as valuable as sand in the Sahara.' Pleased with this literary triumph, he continued, 'Or rock in the Rockies, or salt in the sea, or, or a pork pie in a synagogue.'

'But what about a builder, developer? It could all be flats.'

'What builder wants a court case when he can buy four others in the road with no trouble?'

Benny stood there, blocking the door. The incomprehension on his face confirmed in the agent the theory that he was as thick as two planks, as dull as ditchwater, as . . .

'Look, tell you what. Get rid of the tenant and I'll buy the place for this much,' he wrote a sum, in five figures, on the back of his card and handed it to Benny. 'Okay? A deal?' Although it was several thousand pounds short of the market value of such a house, it was more money than Benny had ever contemplated having, in one go. It would entitle them to emigrate to Australia.

'Yes.'

*

15

'What a nice man that was, Benny. We must have him round to tea one day.'

'Yes, Mother.'

'We could show him our photographs of Aussie. He'd like that.'

'Yes.' Benny tried not to seem preoccupied. 'I think you should ring him up for a date, Mother. The doctor said you should extend your sex life.'

'Oh, Ben, the things tha says!'

She pulled the rug about her knees. Her eyes twinkling. Somewhere in there, Benny thought, was an eighteen-year-old, winking at the world.

'If he saw you in your bikini . . .,' Benny sat next to Bet on the divan, laying out the photographs.

Nightly they do this; poring over them Ben is the essence of patience and keeps alive the Bet-myth that there is no sibling rivalry between himself and Sharon. He the Uncle. As if Uncle were glorious enough a role to make up for his drifting life. And Sharon so rooted, so loved. Sharon always drew love to her as moths to flame, as filings to magnets, gathered it up and gobbled it down. Even Ben's love. You can't *help* loving her. You can tell by the photographs if you didn't know. Sharon consumes the lens, chubby Sharon, as it deifies the two small boys, his nephews.

Groups, all. A group with Sharon and himself, Bet in the middle, shorter but just as round as Sharon, in shorts! He had barely seen his mother's legs, and here they were sparkling with sea water. The sea behind, the sky so blue.

'As blue as . . .,' Benny said.

'Peacock's feathers,' said Bet, 'swimming-pools.' She ran out of comparisons to continue the game.

At night his Northern yard is blue in the sunset, jazzy, jagged metal, blue and sad. The Blues themselves.

Sharon and the children. Sharon's hubbie. There's me in that bathing-suit. Oh, what a sight I am! You're gorgeous, Mother – could pass for twenty any day. Get away with you.

Benny found it hard to play the game. He was distracted, waiting for Margueritte's key in the latch.

*

16

Let's start at the beginning again. Shut your eyes, Mother, can you see those birds, that park again? Oh yes, yes.

'Benny?'

'Mother?'

'Will I ever see it again?'

Benny took her hand. What could he say? He made her so many promises he could not keep. Dying is a state of mind.

'Of course you will.'

But first, I have a few things to do.

2 *Marching Orders*

Margueritte arrived home late, at nearly six-thirty and was due to go out, so she only had ten minutes to spare. They sat opposite each other round the small greasy kitchen table. Margueritte was careful not to let the cuffs of her coat touch anything.

It only took two-and-one-third minutes for Benny to ascertain that Margueritte had no intention of leaving "her" flat, at least not in the forseeable future, was unmoved by his explanation of his mother's life expectancy, and was on firm ground since if he remembered, she had had their contract drawn up by her solicitor friend, and properly witnessed.

'Then I won't accept the rent any more,' Benny said, wildly trying to think of some counter-move.

'Then you shall be the poorer, that's all. 'She got up.' I am unbudgeable. Face up to it. Let's keep things amicable.' She walked out, down the corridor to the stairs, and turned. 'By the way, how is your mother?'

'Worse. She won't be getting any better.'

She looked down at the floor a moment and for one second Benny thought she might relent and his heart quickened.

'Listen,' she said, 'the rent I pay is minimal, I must admit. Up the rent, say ten pounds a week, get the Gas Board to install central heating and put the extra money towards paying it off in instalments. It will add to the value of the property and make life more comfortable for your mother.'

Benny advanced on her down the hall and was pleased to realise, yet again, that he had a good foot over her. She was tiny.

17

'You don't seem t'realise. I want to *sell* the house, not improve it. My mother needs to go back to Australia with my sister and be looked after.'

She turned and started up the stairs, grinning. 'Nonsense,' she said, 'no one could look after her better than you. Just because your sister's a woman doesn't mean she's a better carer. That's just sexism. And all that stuff about health and foreign countries is old hat. They used to send consumptives to Switzerland.'

Benny felt as if he might do something terrible, though he could not think what. He shook. She turned and saw that he was angry.

'Don't be unreasonable, I have my rights. Put yourself in my position.'

Right this is war.

Benedict thought up twelve ways to kill her, enjoying them enormously. Especially the one where he strangled her with a piece of television cable and buried her body under the meters at the far end of the garden. Then he dismissed all twelve and carried his mother tenderly into her own bed.

Benny was not a murderer by nature, not even a criminal by nature. True, he lived so on the margin of society that he had truck with stolen goods from time to time, and was not above cheating big firms (never real people though – he always refused to repossess televisions if a family had them), but this was only as a result of the economic forces currently prevailing in the country. Since the government was an uncaring one, in the opinion of Benny and his drinking companions, which promoted the interests of the privileged few, Benny reacted, like his peers, by developing two moralities: one for dealing with people, and one for dealing with property. Sometimes the two overlapped confusingly, but seldom. Usually it was all too clear what was the obvious thing to do. And also to what extent you kept mum about it.

For example Benny was, statistically, an invisible worker, and in fact owed the government a tremendous amount in back taxes. However, since the NHS doctor on whom he relied was unable, due to government cuts, to provide a district nurse to care for Bet, Benny could not claim to be 'available for work'. He

18

did not see this as contradictory. The state cheats me, and I cheat them. Honour among cheats.

The moral confusion here arises because Margueritte was not what Bet would call 'one of us': she was an individual and yet the issue was property, and even as an individual, she somehow represented to Benny the State. It was probably the Triumph which did it: put her outside the range of his pity. And into the maelstrom of his anger.

And Benny was unaccustomed to expressing anger. Bet had forbidden it, some decades ago. Let no wrath guide you into disaster. Wrath being the Sunday school codeword for anger.

That evening Benny rigged up the buzzer system his sister had given him in Australia, an ingenious device such that should Bet so much as snore loudly, it would switch on and broadcast her every sound. It was called a Kiddy Alert.

With the Kiddy Alert on setting 10, Benny fell into a fitful sleep on the first floor of the house, in between the bottom floor of his mother, and the top floor of Margueritte. Sandwiched between old love and new hate.

3 *Lost in Action*

Every day is another day, the doctor had said. Benny understood this all-encompassing piece of wisdom when he had difficulty rousing Bet from sleep the next morning. For half an instant he thought she was dead and felt the world about him begin to disintegrate. Then she turned towards him and asked for Sharon.

The room where she slept was so cold he decided to put both electric-bar fires on, rather than the temperamental gas for the whole day.

While Mother failed to eat her toast, sitting by the bed on her wicker chair, Ben changed her sheets. She asked whether it was Wednesday then, and he told her that one of the hot-water bottles had leaked in the night. He knew that she did not believe him.

He carried her along to the garden toilet and washed her,

19

propped against the kitchen sink. She let her mind wander, let it ramble and weave about; she spoke of Sharon's Downstairs Cloakroom and he told her she would soon be there, luxuriating in the sit-up bath, or even (giggle, giggle) astride the bidet. He settled her with the Open University and a handy jar of barley sticks 'for the glucose which gives me energy' and got the bike out of the shed behind the toilet.

Roger Rogers and Sons butcher families; they announce so on the cream and bottle-green hip-height tiles on the front of their shop, under the picture window beneath the awning. Sawdust on the floor, frequently wiped white plastic trays of quivering flesh wait in ranks between immortal tufts of dark green paper parsley. The real and the unreal, the dead and the undead.

Roger, or Roger, beneath a real straw hat with specks of blood on the rim, slaps slices onto the scales, smiles, quips, jokes, trims, and wraps the flesh in waxed paper parcels, wiping his hands on the greyest of cloths between scales and cash register. Roger, his son, frowns. Is this any life for a school-leaver who looked forward to a lifetime's unemployment? He doesn't actually have 'I didn't ask to be born' written on his white coat, but it is written on him just the same.

He can't possibly be of any help in any case for the transactions that go on are not in ordinary English, and they are not explicable. Only twenty years' experience will suffice. Meanwhile he minces the inedible bits of sheep families, pig families, cow families and wishes he were somewhere else.

Old ladies come in, bent nearly double and after commenting on the meteorological conditions at Hunter's Bar, not to mention (please don't) Nether Edge, they ask whether he has got anything today.

Can't they see the tubs and trays of meat? Why doesn't Dad ever say, 'Yes, funny you should ask that: *meat*'?

Instead he answers them with one of the following:

a: Not yet but try again tomorrow.

b: I'll go look in the back and see, Mrs X.

c: Got a lovely trotter I can let you have for tenpence.

d: Sorry just give the last to Mrs Y.

The frown on young Roger deepens and deepens.

*

Ben too comments on the weather, together with the customised addition that there will be a few aerials down before the weekend is out.

Then he says his mother is poorly, and, like the elderly, asks whether Roger has anything for him. To which, watched closely by the deeply confused Roger, Roger does a little dance along the chiller, round the chopping block and says, over his shoulder, that Mrs Ashe is in need of a nice piece of beef then.

The curious thing is that no money actually changes hands when Roger has wrapped and presented the small steak.

Ben wheeled his bike down past the Family Butcher, separated from the vegetarians in the health food shop by a knitting shop, past the health food shop to the start of the ten-foot-wide brick cottages out of which those shops had been hewn. About twenty cottages down, there was a gap, a driveway, a high wooden fence with barbed wire on the top: Charlie's fortress. Next door, further down the road, is his video hire shop.

The troops were standing by the back of one of his vans, smoking and sipping at mugs of dark tea.

'Come for my tools,' said Ben. Nobody moved. They were giving the impression of total, eternal inactivity.

'There's no need for that,' said one of them. Only a black youth moved about in the background, gliding a damp chamois leather over the logo 'Charlie's Television Rentals Twenty-Four Hour Troubleshooting' in red on cream.

Here Ben was both the outsider and the blue-eyed boy. Outside the family life on council-house estates they all enjoyed, but the best electronics man, the closed-circuits expert, able even to make small parts from scratch for strange foreign models. They could not brook losing him from the team permanently, even though they harboured a slight envy for his detachment – twice it had come to light that he had been paid 'in kind' by young wives alone during the day (Charlie, usually a fundamentalist in moral matters, looked kindly on the fact that Ben needed an 'outlet' for his natural urges despite or because of his duty to live with his mother) and a half-jesting badinage arose around his exploits as Lancelot to Charlie's Arthur – licensed by virtue of his other, intangible virtues.

21

One of which was his unshakable tolerance in the face of their puns about pluggings-in, good receptions, fusings and so on.

Charlie came out of the office, down the fire-escape metal stairs. A crusty man of middle height with bullet-grey hair and torpedo moustaches. An unlit cigarette gathered dust on his purple lips (he had given up eight years ago).

He handed Ben a cup of tea, asked after his mother, and asked him if he had time to recce down to Chesterfield for some ammo. Ben said no, he had left Mother on her own.

Ben asked his colleagues if any of them were in a position to buy a house, with a sitting tenant. Without exception they were council-housed; in fact Ben was the exception having a property at all. Unmortgageable then, is it? Ben hadn't even thought of that. Yes, perhaps it would be unmortgageable. Then you've got a problem there. Get the lodger to move. Ah, well. Charlie offered, only half in jest, to supply a squadron to 'do over' the lodger. But when Ben pointed out that she was female and a teacher, he withdrew the offer and suggested subterfuge and surprise tactics were more in order. Women, he mused, never fight fair, so you have to mine the approaches.

Charlie sent the commandos into combat with some addresses off a sheet of paper in his hand and put an arm up round Ben's shoulders, leading him up the stairs into the office. Half-way up the stairs he paused to turn and shout, 'Jackets on!' to his men. They wearily let their arms drift into burgundy nylon jackets with the company logo on the front. They would only remove them in the van.

They sat either side of Charlie's desk. Charlie opened drawers, rooted, opened more drawers. Finally he found a small tin box and withdrew ten five pound notes and put them in an envelope.

Benny refused it, sipping his tea. Charlie placed it near him on the desk.

'Think of it as a retainer. Or a loan against future work.'

'No, I'll manage.'

'How? How will you manage?' Benny had already thought this out. He was going to put in a claim for one of those new Attendance Allowances. This, together with Margueritte's rent, would provide enough to live on. Later he would ask Sharon and Ron to send a little money.

Charlie chewed the dead cigarette from one side of his mouth to the other and shook his head.

'Ben, you are a lost man.'

'What?'

'I have lost you.' He swept a hand over his desk, indicating the paperwork on it in random piles. 'You don't exist. I don't pay national insurance for you, you don't pay tax, you don't appear anywhere. You are *lost*, do you understand? Like a soldier lost in action.'

'So? I am entitled. Someone has to look after my mother.'

'Yes, and it has to be you. It is your duty. But you can't claim that you are unable to continue earning money when, technically, you have never earned any.'

'Oh, I see.' Benny took the envelope up and looked at it. What Charlie meant was that he must not get him into trouble with the authorities. Fair enough.

'But I'll take care of you. You're my man. My best,' said Charlie. 'I have a plan.'

He had a new campaign. He was always trying to find ways to beat the opposition into the dust. Last year he had opened a video hire shop along the road and hired out cameras too, so the family could 'immortalise' their kids on film. This year he was leafleting the whole of Sheffield about a Special Service he was offering. Oh yes, said Ben, already worried that he had left Bet on her own too long, but obliged to listen because of the envelope on his lap, what's that then?

Charlie spun out his scheme. What is the chief civilian occupation on Christmas Day? Watching television, Ben advanced. Exactly, well this year we will be On Call for Christmas Day. He had already ordered the paging devices. The pay would be double overtime, cash.

Before he left Ben had agreed to do Christmas Day, even if it meant his mother spending the day with Charlie and his Mrs. As he started down the fire-escape steps Ben heard Charlie call him, asking him why he had returned from Australia at all.

'Heaven knows,' Ben replied.

Cycling home up the steep centre of Sharrow, an area which

23

had become famous since the last census as being the area with the least indoor plumbing in the country, Ben looked at the sky – clouds. Always clouds or rain. Some bricks of the tiny rows of one-up-one-down were still black despite years of Clean Air Acts and anti-pollution protests. The men living out their last days in them had lungs in a similar condition, and their coughing obliterated the natural sounds of birds now anxious to return to the South Yorkshire or North Derbyshire moorland which they had once colonised.

So why come back, and to here, of all places? The logical reason was simply that their permits had run out and the return flight awaited them. But Sharon had put it to him one day at the far end of her garden, where indoor plants stayed out all year and grew monstrous, filtering the light like giant venetian blinds overhead, that they ought to emigrate too.

Ben could only say that he thought Mother was too old to adjust, and left it at that. But the truth was that there was something wrong with Australia which he could not put into words. He had not the abstract nouns at his disposal. But turning from Sharrow into the erstwhile Victorian pretentiousness of Psalter Lane and home, he thought it had something to do with the ground. Here the ground and the air and the lime trees all belonged together. Australia seemed too new a place, and the people too concerned about *things*. Sharon herself had changed – it wasn't just the accent which tinged her speech but stained her sons' completely – it was more than that. Perhaps, and Benny could not quite put it into words, the place still seemed colonial, developing.

'Nice place to visit,' Bet had said, 'but not to live.'

Still, he was prepared to go now, if it meant Bet, who was only sixty-four, might live into her nineties, sitting in the shade of Sharon's garden, watching her grandsons grow.

The macaroni cheese Ben cooked Bet for lunch looked uncannily like steak.

'Ah! the power of the imagination,' said Ben, cutting up her meal.

She asked Benny when the first people would start to arrive to see the house. Any minute now, he said, shall I put your corset on?

'It wouldn't suit you,' she said, as he had hoped. Where there is corn, there is . . .

While she napped, he fitted the new lock on the front door. It took him over an hour, since he had to scoop out more wood to fit the new lock, and had only screwdrivers and no chisel to do it with.

He did not really expect this lock to keep Margueritte *out* for long, and was certain that this was not the solution, but he did it in the spirit of harassing her, making her feel unwelcome, letting her know that he was in earnest. The work was finished about half an hour before the earliest possible time she could be home.

Mother was watching a quiz show in which the contestants had to find the most banal endings to the beginning of phrases. If they showed the least ingenuity or intelligence, they forfeited the new Ford parked on stage, when he looked out of the windows and saw, in the rain, her car draw up. He turned up the volume of the television.

'Can't hear what they're sayin', Mother.'

Mother could not hear the door shaking and rattling as Margueritte tried to open it with her key. Just as well. He wouldn't want to have to explain. This smacked of landlords evicting innocent families, or unfairness, or even violence. The rattling stopped and she went away. Perhaps she would stay with a friend. A friend who would say, perhaps, that it might be better to start looking for alternative accommodation.

In less than an hour she was back, with reinforcements. Benny had not expected this. It was that bloke of hers, the only one who had ever stayed the night. Furnace he was called, or something like that. He had heard the fond farewells in the morning, snooping, under the stairs.

When Furnace rang the bell loudly, three times, Mother was startled and was sure that it was people come to view the house. Benny was thus hoist on his own petard and had to answer the door.

It was Furnace.

Benny let them in out of the rain.

'It's all right, Mother,' he called out, 'it's only Margueritte and her fancy man,' knowing Margueritte would not like that.

Furnace came right in, motioning Margueritte to go straight upstairs.

'Check your locks,' he said. 'Where can we speak, Mr Ashe?' he asked.

'Doesn't thy voice work in't hall?' said Benny, trying to make it clear that they had nothing to say to each other by putting on the local yokelspeak.

Furnace frowned. He was trying to look older, sound more important. He plunged his hands into his jacket pockets and swayed about.

'I know how you feel,' he began.

'Do you?' asked Benny, astonished. 'Your mother dying is she, for want of a few thousand?'

The door into Mother's room, the television blaring, was open nearby. Benny shut it gently and led Furnace down the corridor to the small kitchen. Furnace followed him, trying not to let his eyes rest on the dilapidation all around him. Benny was a big man, and seemed even larger in the small room. There was something odd about his face. From the front it seemed coarse, bulbous even, but his profile was classic, sharp. For a moment, but only one moment, for Furnace believed all Englishmen were basically gentlemen, he feared for Margueritte's physical safety. Andrew Furness looked at the chairs and decided to stand. His suit had cost several hundred pounds and cleaning it cost five.

'Look, Mr Ashe, you can't go changing the locks every time you fall out with a tenant. It's against the law.'

'You the fuzz, then?'

'No, solicitor.'

'Going to set the law on me, are ya?'

'No. But I will do whatever is necessary to protect Margueritte. I'm sure you can understand that. Imagine if someone was threatening your mother.'

'I don't have to imagine that.'

'I mean in actual *fact*, offering physical violence to your mother.'

'Oh. I didn't realise. Margueritte is your mother, is she?'

'Don't be abstruse. I'm referring to protecting the weaker sex.'

26

'Sex?' said Benny, smiling horribly. What did abstruse mean? Suddenly the noise of the television penetrated down the hall. Mother was inching out of the room on her two sticks. Benny pushed angrily past Furnace and went to her.

'Mother! What you up to?'

'I want to show them around my floor,' she began, nearly toppling. Benny led her back into her room.

'Here have the keys, sod you. Give one to Her. She's got to go, so I can sell this house. Now go.'

'This harassment has got to stop,' shouted Furnace, as Benny shut the door on him. Andrew Furness, Benny would have been astonished to know, had been almost trembling with fright during this 'unpleasantness', but now felt unaccountably brave.

There's nothing unaccountable about it – all chickens become rams when the restraining influence of a Mother turns up, however frail.

Benny put away the photographs and helped Bet to sip her hot milk, in her bedroom, sitting on the edge of the bed.

'Mother. Could you do something for me?'

'Yes, anything, dear.'

'I want you to ask Margueritte to leave.'

'Why? She can leave when the house is sold. Or she can stay and the new people will have the rent. That's all right.'

Benny sighed. How could he tell her, without alarming her? 'It will be hard for us to sell the house with her sitting in it. People want to have the house empty, completely.'

'Then give her notice. That's what we always did. Gave them notice.'

'I have. But she won't go.'

Bet was not stupid, and now it dawned on her. 'That's a new law, is it?'

'Yes,' said Benny, 'but I thought if you asked her, she might agree to it.'

Bet slumped down in the bed, her face fallen.

'Well?' said Benny.

'It's no good,' Bet said, 'she isn't one of us.'

'But woman to woman, you know.'

Bet laughed feebly. 'That's not a woman, son. If she were a

27

real woman she'd be married, and had kiddies be now. Like our Sharon.'

Bet was right, of course. There was no common ground on which they could both stand, on which he could make an appeal which would strike home.

Or rather, such was the gap there that Benny could not think of any.

For two weeks Benny tried ingenious little ways to get her to leave. His one and only parameter was that he always stopped short of violence. He got her phone cut off by the Post Office; she had it reconnected, and the number ex-directory.

He removed the fuses supplying the overhead lights, but she replaced them herself and put a note by the box saying, 'Don't do this, Mr Ashe, I warn you: I will tell the police.'

And during this time Bet became weaker and weaker. The fires raged all night in her room, which she never left now. Benny lengthened the TV cable so she could watch from bed, but her eyes were usually closed.

The hot-water bottles leaked every night now. At first Benny made incontinence jokes to cheer her up – centring largely on the odd coincidence that incontinence supplies were called AIDS which was also the name of an epidemic among sexually active people which even Bet had heard of. Gradually the jokes wore as thin as tissue and Benny stopped them and spoke of Australia always, and Sharon's house. He learnt to describe it as if they were walking around it, room by room. She would squeeze his hand and murmur.

He spoke to her of the waves, the warmth, the sand. She smiled, her eyes tight closed against the bone-cruel Sheffield autumn, dreaming of Perth.

On the night of the ninth of November at four o'clock in the morning the Kiddy Alert screeched and whistled, Benny jumped out of bed and was with Bet in one minute. She was having a seizure. From the phone near her bed, with her in his arms, twitching and shaking, he phoned for an ambulance.

28

Bet died in the ambulance, in Benny's arms.

One minute she was looking straight at him and quite suddenly though her eyes did not shut, the life went out of them.

4 *Into the Tank*

One way or another Benny was in the hospital all morning, waiting for papers to be signed, or people to be contacted by phone. He made a call himself, long distance, reversing the charges, to Sharon. She cried on the phone. Benny envied her. She would cry for hours and Ron would hold her and hold her and not let her go, and she would recover, and start to make them all a meal, take up the meaningful threads of her genuine full life once more.

Before she rang off, through the sobs, she said, 'Ben dear, come to us when you can. Always welcome. We love you.'

Sharon spoke with a broad Australian accent now.

Benny did not cry. He sat, waiting, in a corridor near Casualty. The ambulance driver brought him a cup of tea and made so bold as to offer him some comfort. At least your mother died quick, he said, not like mine who was in pain for eight months, paralysed. Didn't know us at the end.

What did Bet know at the end?

What was death really? Was just the set turned off perhaps, though the video still ran, recording . . . what? Where?

Benny felt as if he had broken something like a sound barrier into real life, for even men in uniform were suddenly sons, or fathers, or potential fathers. Even the nurses were real, just women. Not that it was any comfort – on the contrary, it was frightening.

Ben walked all the way home, up avenue after avenue of arthritic trees jerking in the wind and dropping dead leaves under the dead grey sky. He sat in the kitchen and waited for Margueritte to come home.

When she did, she came straight into the kitchen and stood in front of him.

'That was a stupid trick. Your dumbest yet.'

'What?'

'Redirecting my post. How could you?'

Benedict stared at her. She had earrings in the shape of moons, silver moons on little chains made of stars. Later, and for the rest of his life, these earrings figured as giant engines in his nightmares.

'How did you find out?'

'It was a real address you sent them to and they'd opened a letter from the Income Tax and it had my home address there.'

Benny laughed. 'I thought it was a good one. Very good. It might have worked.'

Her face darkened and the earrings swayed and projected the light from the fluorescent tube above them over the wall behind him.

She turned to go upstairs. She had not asked about Mother. Benny followed her up, three stairs behind. He must tell her about Mother.

At the turning of the stair she faced him. That point where the estate agent had suffered a small internal crisis.

'What do you *want*? What is it now?'

'I want to talk to you.'

'What about?' She walked the last few stairs and turned the key in her lock. Benny pushed past her to prevent her entering the flat.

'My Mother died this morning.'

Let us pause here. In case there is, out there in the cosmos, anything more than plasma, black holes, gas explosions, curved infinity of radioactivity and atomic vastness, anything *conscious* or judgemental, I wish to make the cases for the two participants, at this, the most crucial intersection of their lives, perfectly clear.

Or, put more simply – Bet, can you hear me?

Margueritte has had a gruelling day (more of this later, and via a most unexpected route) and has suffered two weeks of excruciating harassment from Benedict, her hitherto quite reasonable landlord. It is also day two of a most horrendous period, during which plasma, black holes and an infinity of atomic vastness in the form of red lumps have been abandoning her body for no apparent reason, though she would be the last person to cite this

30

as an excuse; I do. Now she hears that the indirect source of her harassment has passed on to that Eternal Tenancy in the Sky and finds it hard to disguise her relief. Who wouldn't?

Benedict has not cried, but he is ready to. The loss of his mother is something no one in the universe can quite understand. Even those of us who have lost mothers cannot quite grasp the uniqueness of his suffering. We cannot even begin. But some aspects of his state of mind are universal: since the loss seems to him as unnecessary as the loss of a child to the parents of a murder victim, he is finding it difficult to *forgive*. But forgiveness is in his nature, since he is a normal, mature adult. He has learnt to forgive – but for forgiveness to be triggered there first has to be *contrition*. The perpetrator must be *sorry* for what they have done, or seem to have done.

If Margueritte softens for a moment (are you listening, black holes?) and gives even the slightest hint of remorse, Benny will forgive her. He wants to forgive her.

Then he can cry.

'Then all your troubles are over and you can stop harassing me, can't you?' said Margueritte, pushing past him into her flat.

To his credit, perhaps, Benedict did not strike her, nor force his way into the flat. He said nothing, but his heart turned to stone; or rather, to put it more scientifically, his desire to forgive was transmuted into hatred and that hatred was to find relief only in revenge.

Benny sat until twelve in Bet's armchair, fighting down waves of nausea or pain or anxiety by strength of will, and thinking. He could not weep. He could not get up. The effort of not crying took all his concentration. A paralysis of the spirit possessed him.

He climbed up slowly to his room, where he undressed the body he was trapped in and slipped it between the sheets. Leaving it there he went and stood by the window, looking out.

Perhaps it does not matter now? Or perhaps it matters more than ever? He looked down over the darkening avenue of Psalter Lane, always dark because of the lime trees, always damp (so unlike Australia), and a plan the size of an army tank moving down the street took hold of him. Before falling asleep, he had entered the tank and heard with extreme pleasure (or consolation) the steel door closing overhead.

5 *The Craters of the Moon*

Benny hears the front door shutting. Margueritte has gone to work. Benny has had a whole night's uninterrupted sleep and feels dizzy and confused with the heady sense of life flooding into him. He had not realised how short of sleep he had been over the last few months.

Neither does he know how effective is a dose of pure hatred for activating the body. Not for nothing does an American football coach whip his men into a fury of hatred before sending them onto the field.

He shaves and washes and eats a hurried piece of toast.

On the landing, about where the estate agent had stood, realising that the gem of a house was unsaleable, Benny takes a look over his shoulder as if someone in the gloom is following him.

No one is.

Her door opens to let out a waterfall of light. As if he had opened a stage door. Benny stands, blinking, in a room which at first seems to be a small forest. For he is aware only of blinding light and the large leaves of a jungle.

This is the top of my house but it is a foreign country, another planet.

Neil Armstrong must have gazed up at the moon many times before going there. He knew what it was. You can't walk, run, court, sing under the moon without wondering and deciding what it *is*. So when he visited it, he saw what he had expected to see – rocks, ground. They probably told him at astronaut school in NASA, 'You will see rocks and ground.' Who is to say that what he saw was any more than a figment of his education? When we see nine straight lines so joined as to give the three-dimensional impression of a cube, we say, confidently, 'that is a cube'. But it isn't. It's just nine lines on a piece of paper. But

32

we are educated to look for shapes and interpret them. There are people somewhere on earth who have never seen a cube and would say, in some other language, 'they are marks on paper', confidently.

So someone having gone to the moon doesn't help. We each need to go for ourselves.

So here is Benny, uneducated, with no preconceptions, testing the gravity on Margot's territory, and trying to interpret it.

He has not been trained for this expedition and so a primeval fear of being found in the wrong place makes Benny behave like a primitive. He shuts the door and backs up to it; his back is protected – he has, as it were, a line back to the capsule. For a point of reference, he looks down at his feet. Underneath is polished wood. Not carpet or linoleum, but *wood*. His eyes, half lidded still against the light, for here he is closer to the sun and above the lime thickets, follow the line of the shiny board to a – rug is it? Scattered about the large room are large squares of white felt with pink pictures on them. The felt is frayed all round the edges as if, as if a fight happened here?

What does happen here, really? What room is this? The function is unclear. There is no television, so it can't be the sitting-room. And yet there is a sofa, pink leather, floppy with two buttons. There are two enormous cushions with pink and grey stripes on the floor, a standard lamp in the shape of a giant tulip bending over the sofa; in front a smoked-glass-topped coffee table with magazines beneath, the only sign of disarray.

Turning to his left Benny sees the desk, again of polished, pale wood, with a pedestal of drawers, and on it a metal lamp curving from nowhere, from the wall.

There is a small portable typewriter near the front edge of the desk. His own address is neatly typed in the top right-hand corner of the one piece of paper poking up from the roll; and then, below, 'Dear Mother,'. Above this are shelves full of paperbacks, rows and rows. Hundreds. Stretching along the wall to the – what, bathroom? kitchen?

Crossing the room Benny lowers the blinds. Having looked out

33

of the french windows onto the balcony and seen, for nearly the first time, the *tops* of the lime trees outside.

Now the light inside is suffused, beige and pink.

Benny explores the kitchen, and is amazed to find wooden implements where he thought only plastic was available, red ceramic sets, machines, a microwave oven, two bar stools and a breakfast bar. On the walls a small red fleur-de-lis sprigged everywhere. Bottles of wine are slotted horizontally into a rack at floor level. There is a small fridge and a small freezer, fully stocked. Vegetarian cookbooks on a pine shelf.

Her magazines are not ones he had ever read aloud to Bet. There is *Cosmopolitan, She,* a legal magazine, *Spare Rib,* the *Observer Magazine,* and a few copies of the *Guardian.* Benny sits on the pink leather sofa and leafs through some of them. They are actually very similar to Bet's magazines only glossier, and aimed at a smarter woman.

Rather than looking for Slimmer of the Month, they look for the new Fay Weldon. Not knowing who the old Fay Weldon was, Benny cannot comprehend this. Neither can he interpret the recipes in these books, which employ ingredients he has never heard of or seen in shops.

There is a problem page with questions about sex, but the problems are more complicated, often involving at least one married man and a lesbian. There are still horoscopes, but they exhort the reader to remain firm where work partners make difficulties rather than to smooth over family rows; still items about clothes, only it isn't how to make them, knit them, crochet them, but where to buy them. And judging by the prices listed near the pictures (in which the model's face is more prominent than the clothes advertised, which are always whirling away somewhere out of the picture on a windy day) the reader is earning upwards of half a million pounds a month. The articles about babies are about how to conceive them without a husband, breastfeed them, teach them to read, rather than how to knit and crochet for them.

Same old stuff about Princess Diana too, only it is where she goes for dresses rather than what hospitals she has opened and what she might have said to Mrs X on ward eight.

Benny tries to summon up the Average Reader in an attempt

to understand Margueritte. She is unmarried though with count-less lovers, male and female, she does not knit, is outrageously wealthy and has a job in the City, holidays in Turkey for which she lays out several thousand on clothes which will look sufficiently ethnic. On the other hand she has a definite weight problem and will only cook meals to which a calorie count has been added.

Next Benny investigates a stack of equipment with a smoked glass door which seemed to be, on inspection, a record player, a radio tuner, and a twin cassette tape recorder.

Her records: she has various operas with German or Italian names, four Joni Mitchell albums, Patti Smith, Bruce Springsteen, Vivaldi (the *Four Seasons*), *Porgy and Bess* and an ornately decorated poetry reading by John Betjeman called *Late Flowering Love*. Ben has heard of Mozart and Haydn of course, though he cannot remember when, and she seems to have several dozen of these.

The bedroom is wallpapered with mirrors: one wall has mirrors with knobs and proves to be a wall-length wardrobe.

In the middle of the room is a king-sized bed with black sheets.

Here he finds the television too, a small portable set which none the less has a video underneath it and a box of cassettes next to it. Benny turns it upside-down to see if there are any stickers on it, whether anyone has ever repaired it. Nothing. There are some tapes she has recorded herself and the title (BBC or C4) is written on the label and the date and title of the piece. She has recorded mostly well-known films.

Two hired videos (not from Charlie's) called *Ready and Willing* and *The Plumber* are hidden behind the rack.

Her clothes are not such a surprise. After all he has seen quite a few of them, though he had never bothered much to observe them as closely as he does now.

Very little synthetic material. Cotton, silk, wool. Hundreds of shoes, many of them patent, and boots. Ski outfits, bikinis. Suits, silk blouses. Jewellery hung on the door, all colour-organised. She liked enamelware, and ethnic beads.

One thing he cannot account for: the two hundred or so boxes of dried and UHT milk at one end. Does she daily expect war to break out?

Benny feels hot, a little dizzy in this place. He feels along the silk sheets, stops himself, leaves the room and sits down at the desk. Above him the books. Bob Geldof, *The Joy of Sex* (fancy daring to buy it in a shop; or did The Furnace give it to her?), some Graham Greene novels, Kate Millett *Sexual Politics* (no pictures), a large book in two volumes called OED, a book of nudes called *The History of Photography*, a medical encyclopaedia.

More books than anyone could ever read. Benny was not one for reading or writing.

But he had, like many semi- or non-literate people, a gift for detailed memorising. He had once joked to Charlie that should he be struck blind he would still be able to work, since he would be able to tell someone else exactly what to expect in the guts of a television, down to the last screw and diode. There was not one item belonging to Margueritte which he had seen, which he would forget. Whereas she, if asked to describe him, would have had difficulty being accurate.

In the desk drawers Benny finds letters, documents, passport, income tax files, even a copy of the contract between his mother and Ms M. Mason, upon which he smiles ruefully. He is just about to stop his searching when a small hard-backed notebook noses up towards his hand, from the very back of the middle drawer. He draws it out, together with all the papers that had been on top of it, so that he can put it back convincingly.

It is her diary. Normally reading someone else's diary would be that sort of despicable thing which Benny would not do. But this is out and out warfare and he needs to know the Opposition. So far she had all the advantages, those of education, knowledge, wealth, the Law (in the shape of Furnace), and probably Influential Friends. Benny has this diary, and a key to her flat. If living always on the fringes of poverty has taught Benedict anything, it has taught him how to exploit what little there is.

On the first page it has, printed in black, Collins Page At A View Diary 1986, and a list of personal details, date of birth, height, weight, nationality, National Insurance number. But of much
36

more significance to Benny, she has filled every page of the diary with small writing, slanting slightly forwards. Benny takes the diary, and spreads it out in front of him at the desk, rests his head in his hands and prepares himself to memorise as much of the contents as possible.

6 *Diary 1*

Sunday 19th October (end half-term)
All through half-term it has been coming upon me that I cannot live my life on the off-chance, as most people do. On the off-chance that the nearest (and how staggeringly near it *is*) nuclear power-station will not blow a gasket, that the microwave oven will not rearrange the molecules of my bloodstream in such a way that when I am eighty I shall be forced to peer eternally through the square, smoked-glass lenses of my once-eyes, while anchored to a kitchen surface. Or that Dorothea will have a final all-encompassing nervous breakdown to end all breakdowns, kill herself and leave her English Dept Scale 4 vacant for me at last; or that Andrew F. has never slept, in his boyish innocent way, with four gay drug abusers who have incipient AIDS. Or that I will not catch it because I shower so frequently.

I have got to be safe. Of what am I sure?

That if Dorothea dies I shall inherit the headship. The flip side of this is that although she smokes forty a day and bottles out every few weeks, she is in rude health otherwise and I wait on this miserable pay scale eternally.

That I am a secure Sitting Tenant (Andrew F. says) and cannot be evicted.

That Andrew F. is reasonably faithful.

Though I am looking forward to seeing the children (and some staff) again, and am fully prepared to work hard, I here resolve to do as often as possible the thing which secures my safety.

Monday 20th October
Today the first day back – chaos. I had prepared to continue teaching same sets, but found had to cover for maths teacher and my O Level Eng. third stream has become fifth year non-exam due to Dorothea's 're-think'. Also Head asked me to supervise

37

swimming of second form on Thurs p.m.s. To show willing seemed keen. Mentioned Drama Club needs to be rescheduled. Have to drop that, he said, since Studio now Maths Room.

Policeman roaming the upper gallery above sports hall. J. says he checking on radical lefty teachers doing sex lessons and Peace Studies. You don't do that, do you, he asked. Don't know, I said, within earshot Dorothea – have to check today's timetable. Dorothea (later lunch queue) in good form, though. Dpty. Head (bald spiv geog.) pushed in front of her for coffee trolley. 'I hope you don't think having a dongly thing means you're entitled to supersede me in the queue!' He red, retired. Must say, will miss her when she dies. Please God, how long?

Mr Ashe wandering about in gloomy back garden with teapot when got home this p.m. Why on earth did they come back from Austr.?

Old lady is brown – looks almost human. Can't say same for son; pasty-faced, middle-aged yob. Andrew says don't trust him, he's probably Hitchcock-type psycho dressing up as dead mother! Nothing so interesting is my guess. But he does seem to dote on the old hag.

Letter from Inland Revenue about my 'floating whale' – still adrift. Wrote back with Rocket. Drift = Stop bothering me or I'll stop paying income tax. Andr. says have no leg to stand on. Whales too are legless, I quipped. Talk of legs etc, I agreed Wednesday his place.

Unplugged microwave. Is it moral to offer it for sale on school noticeboard?

Tuesday 21st October
Migraine a.m. Saw Angela bolting trampoline with sixth formers (all much bigger than her) and cancelled jogging. She shovelled me into her equipment room where she smokes to be vitupera-tive about some chap refusing to use Durex (AIDS) and what did I think – she had thrown him out small hours of morning into the rain?! She seemed v. proud of this 'self-control' as she called it. I said her life sounded somewhat sordid. She said beggars can't be choosers and she was nearly twenty-eight!
38

Dorothea has decided we must teach the non-exam pupils how to fill in VAT forms and how to spell their own addresses. Does she think they are all going to have their own businesses?

Wednesday 22nd October
Due to inability to see other than small area in front of me (tunnel) had to wait for ergotomine to work and late for assembly. Dorothea bitterly sardonic (or bloody rude) about docking the fifteen minutes off my annual free afternoon, and assigning me extra playground duty. Pointed out had worked late five nights this term already, also swimming supervision, drama club, classical studies for morons, remedial English for Sec. Six etc. She not impressed. I didn't get where I am today by not doing a little extra-mural stuff. Not as if you have children of your own like some of us.

Ooooh where is that bus which will run her down???????????
Bald Spiv (geog.) showed us a map of British Isles without Sheffield on it. This meant to be humour. Andrea (slotting St Moritz into holder with flourish) said goes to show that there is hope for her nil-intelligence, non-exam fourth years — they can become geographers.

Perhaps they stood on the North Circular, shaded their eyes with a hand, and peered north. They would miss it then. Because whenever you come 'home' to here, there's a crest, you travel upwards and then suddenly in front of you is the whole hilly basin, in a depression before you. A wonderful view in; but none out. There is a way out west, through the famous Snake Pass, frozen and shut all winter, to Manchester. But otherwise it seems cut off, here inland, furthest from the sea that you can get in England.

If only the Russians had based their maps on this map, we would be on no target lines, no bomb-range. And the nuclear fires could rage over England and pass us by, the Depression, the hills protecting us. We could construct a dome from Dore to Tinsley — a circle which would rise up in two halves and seal us from the atmosphere. Sheffield will then sink down into the disused mines of its past, towards its spiritual home.

I won't mind. I have still a year's supply of alternative milk in the bedroom.

I would only pity the botanical gardens, withering under the plexiglass of a flame-red sky turned off.

Dinner *chez* Andrew – he v. boring about new car. *4/10. Andrew thinks that: a) the only thing that has stopped the Russians from invading Europe in the last forty years is our Nuclear Deterrent, and b) that the amount of radiation we received in the spring during what I call the Passover was equivalent to eating one and a half Brazil nuts a year.

Thursday 23rd October
Have removed Brazil nuts from Muesli.

Held Drama Club in Physics Lab. They want to have real fire (Bunsen burners) on stage. Said would consider it. Such enthusiasm, born no doubt of having to improvise surroundings. Dorothea vetoed fire – said I would never become Head of any Dept by trusting the children.

   Told J. He said, why don't you put in for Head of Drama? Only drawback – no Drama Department to be head of. Technicality, he says. Wait till you're qualified, I said, then you'll take it all more seriously.

   Suddenly thought: what will we do when he leaves in June? Hire somebody? There is no money for string to tie the O Level papers in, Dorothea says, they have each got to bring four inches of the stuff with them in June.

Friday 24th October
Sent two boys (Jerry and Damian) to Bald Spiv (geog.) for chastising since they insulted Sandra – 'Sandra's Mother is a Whore' they wrote on board. Later they were singing it! Afterwards had talk with Sandra, about sticks and stones etc., was there anything I could do? Shocked when she said quite calmly, it's OK her mother *is* a prostitute. How do you know? Everyone knows.

   Everyone but me. I don't seem to know anything any more. Told Dorothea this info – what should I do? She – Why do you insist on prying into their private lives? They will only retaliate by prying into yours.

40

Sinister! D. has poisonous view of world because her own soul is poisonous.

Sunday 26th October
If only I could have a baby on spec. See if it works out. Who would be the father. Andrew? J.? Bald Spiv (geog.)? Oh, God, the thought of having to see some chap every day for the foreseeable future . . .

Angela phoned. Told her was thinking of dropping Andrew. Can I have him then, she said. (Does she mean it?) Sure, I said, but I may need him back, now and then.

Best sort of men are now and then men, we agreed. Sometimes think Angela has a wisdom beyond her years.

Played *Springsteen Live* v. loudly (hope landlord and his mother thoroughly distressed) and danced about like twit.

Monday 27th October
Angela after assembly asked whether I minded if she went to a party with Andrew. That was quick work! When did I introduce them? Must have been the sixth form hop last term. No, I said, course not.

Damn. Why am I so *nice*? Angela isn't. She won't stop at . . .

Played my Heifetz (Bruch) which always expresses my sharpest, most painful experiences. Is there anyone in the world who could listen to this, or to the last song of choirboy whose voice is breaking, and not be moved? Only someone with no emotions at all.

Tuesday 28th October
Soggy sky and winds all day. Sheffield so steep everywhere the wind gets you upside-down as it were.

Saw Angela lunchtime. Had *super* time, she said. Quite revived her confidence in humanity. Andrew so witty, etc. Did they? 'Now that's for me to know, and you to wonder at.' What kind of a stupid thing is that to say?

Ran into the landlord-type moron by the dustbins. He says his mother is not well.

41

Think he is either a dustman or some sort of miner. Are there still miners here? There seemed to be a pit-head on the moors when we went on the school trip to a stately home. I presumed it was a museum piece.

Wednesday 29th October
Andrew phoned to cancel movies.

Dorothea has lost key to book cupboard and pointed out that photocopying teacher's copies was illegal. This hardly affects her since all her senior forms have their *own* books, but J. and I are buggered.

Thursday 30th October
J. broke lock to store cupboard during assembly (gave me the *Kes* I have been desperate for) and then scarpered.

Dorothea has called police. J. and I conspired to ignore this. It seems J. is due to be 'seen' this afternoon by his tutor and cannot manage without copies of something. His whole career depends on it, he said.

Friday 31st October
Under fierce questioning from cops, said I had seen Damian and Jerry hanging about near store cupboard yesterday morning. Altho this is not true, feel it is some sort of Natural Justice. Still, wish J. had owned up.

Dorothea says this is a good sign since it must mean that the rougher element in the school put some premium on the contents of the cupboard, which is only books.

It is agreed that nothing is missing because the boys were disturbed.

J.'s tutor gave him thumbs up.

Saturday 1st November
Andrew came round with wine. Drank all afternoon. Videos etc. ** nearly 6/10, but then he went abruptly leaving me to sleep off effects of wine, and for a moment in the half light of the bedroom I thought I saw someone else in the mirror by the wardrobe and felt suddenly frightened and alone. Don't go, I said. I must, he said. I'm going to a concert.

Fuck him!

With Angela?

He – speech about how we are free and independent humanoids with own lives etc. I invented all this stuff, he said, so why change now. No, only kidding, I said, anyway I told Angela to take an interest in you, I said, to annoy him. Instead he said very grateful because they get on so well. He feels they kindred souls etc.

Yuk.

Men.

Monday 3rd November – My b/day
Dorothea has found keys to storeroom in her handbag (the Other One).

Angela avoided me in assembly and thereafter, just as well, felt would bite off heads. Dorothea congratulated me on lunchtime production by Junior Drama held in hall (the fire looked so realistic, she said). I wouldn't have minded Andrew forgetting, but it was Dorothea giving me a little card with a lady policeman on it and 'Best wishes, from the ogre' inside which broke me up. Andrew could have given me flowers at least.

Cards from mother, bought in aid of some godforsaken Born Again sect in Bournemouth; also letter Inland Rev saying I owe them eight hundred pounds and forty-nine pence, and they will start proceedings. Just let them try.

Oh, God, please send me next year for my birthday a man, early thirties, strong, simple (a farm labourer, gamekeeper, shepherd) but with extreme good looks (something like Olivier as Heathcliff, or the young Lawrence of Arabia), with an enormous sex drive, private means and a great desire for children, which he will not expect me to care for exclusively. A small estate in Derbyshire (ten acres, no more, own milk and cheese) from where I can commute to a private girls' school where I will be teaching them a little Byron and T. S. Eliot for A Level.

'I'll never understand thee, Margot', he will say, 'but that duzzna matter. Tha'll do for me, and I'll do for thee and forgive thee always.'

Stuff like that.

When I got in this evening Benedict (saw his name on a letter

43

from Australia – funny I always thought he was a Bert) said Doctor had been to his mother. Surely he ought to expect this from now on – she must be in her late zillions!

Tuesday 4th November
Andrew apologised forgetting my b/day. Offered take me for dinner. Accepted after suitable hesitation – said wanted to speak to him about my Floating Whale now about to become a Legal Issue. Then he commuted the sentence to drinks after work, as he remembered an appointment.

During drinks – Big Confession. Must admit I was shocked. Try to be open-minded. Apparently Angela thinks quite 'normal' but insisted on blood test for AIDS. Glad to get away. Desperate to have shower with Dettol. For God's sake how much bodily fluid do you need to swap, or not?

Don't think about this.

On top of everything when I came home Benedict steered me into his disgusting kitchen (salmonella, rabies?) and *made* me listen to a ridiculous attempt at an eviction. He thinks his mother needs to go back to Austr. Because of her health. Says doctor told him. Offered him money for central heating. He quite stupid; doesn't understand the issues.

Douched with Dettol: exquisitely painful!

Wednesday 5th November
Landlord has gone mad! He had locks changed on front door. Had to get Andrew (shit) to support me. Feared physical violence; also wanted a witness anything should happen. Andrew gave him talking to and left. We have nothing to say to each other. This saddens me.

However – happy thought: hope Benedict will catch AIDS from arguing with Andrew F.

Could not sleep until fireworks had died down.

Thursday 6th November
Hard to concentrate. Wrote thank-you letter to mother for cheque on staffroom WP. Dorothea that glazed pre-breakdown look. Did not fail to point out how peaky she looked. She said she thinks she has diabetes. Definitely the pre-stages.

Angela (sheepish) approached during lunchbreak and said her

women friends more important to her than mere blokes and would I come to dinner with her and her new flatmate this evening. Suspect Andrew has already sunk to 4/10!

Had dinner (awful spaghetti bol. and rasp. ripple ice-cream) with Angela and her flatmate. Black girl (Sally), single parent. Mostly discussed her probs with housing etc. The baby in a carry-cot by our side. Didn't move. They sleep all the time apparently. Later she took him out of the cot and breastfed him. Found this somehow disgustingly interesting. You don't see it much these days.

Will that generation all die of AIDS?

I don't feel safe in anyway now. Landlord insane; sex-life non-existent; work tedious.

P.M. Tried phoning Andrew for news. Phone temperamental.

Friday 7th November
Dorothea absent. Why nobody minds her unreliability, but when it's *me*?

Found out my phone been disconnected. Must be the mad Benedict again. Explained to British Telecom (after all I'm a shareholder) and have now ordered an ex-directory number which I won't write on the machine. Thinks he can out-fox me? Never!

Saturday 8th November
I should have guessed. Benedict was skulking about by the door to the cellar this morning when I came back from the supermarket. He was obviously buggering the fuses for my flat, because the electricity was out by three o'clock. I have fuse wire. No problem, but I left a message for him, saying would call the police if this happens again. I hope he can read. I only used little words.

Party at J.'s p.m. Told several people about Mad B. No one interested. Either they think I'm inventing it or obsessed. I await his next trick with a mixture of curiosity and rage. My life is now reduced to waiting for the sick landlord's next trick. How pitiful.

Monday 10th November
This has been, without doubt, one of the worst days of my life so far. Why do I say so far? Do I expect worse? No, there is none. First of all my newly repaired phone rang at seven-thirty in the

45

morning and it was Jerry Smith from the fourth form non-ex. saying that he had two letters addressed to me and readdressed their house. His mum had opened one he said, to see if there were any address (*was*, Jerry, not were) and one was from the Income Tax and had it on, so he was phoning to say his mum would give them me if I came by 'cause she didn't want him to take them to school. This number is ex-directory, I said, puzzled. Oh, his mum knows a girl on the switchboard at Central Switching and she simply dialled the number without giving it out.

I dressed and rushed round, before school.

In the car I read them, outside Jerry's house. The one from the I.R. was note to tell me of the Proceedings which were now underway . . . but the other one was Andrew telling me the AIDS test was negative. Elation mixed with Utter Horror – Mrs Smith had read this? Had Jerry too? Would the whole school shortly be writing, 'Miss Mason's boyfriend had an AIDS test' on the boards of every room I enter. I almost cried.

All through assembly I weighed up whether to take horrible Jerry into my confidence and ask him, a) whether he read it, and b) what it would take to silence him if he did. Money? Straight As? Decided to own up to breaking into store room to get Jerry off the hook.

This is all Angela's fault. Though *she* didn't redirect my mail. That must have been Benedict. Worked this out during third year Eng.

On the other hand I won't die of AIDS. Not sure if this is a good thing any more.

Immediately after assembly Head beckoned me into his (sumptuous) 'orifice' as J. calls it to hand me bunch of test papers from Dorothea's upper sixth classes (*Childe Harold's Pilgrimage*, which I have not read) and explained to me that she was now in hospital with a Nervous Breakdown and would be there for at least three weeks. In view of the fact that I am the next senior member of the English Department I would have to take it upon me to fill the gaps. This entails marking all her tests (which have been mounting up in her short absence) and covering all her upper classes. He would take it upon himself to make any administrative decision needed of course (of course, I get no *power* just the extra work) and I would be excused swimming supervision,

46

Drama Club and two lunchtime duties a week. Big deal! This should give me one extra hour to do Dorothea's job. My mouth must have fallen open.

Went and sat in staffroom blinking, then remembered J. minding the first form for me. Went to relieve him. He says he would like to help but has never read *any* Byron, nor taught a sixth form. They don't let him, he says. He can't do my lunch duties either because of football.

While raiding Tampax machine in girls' toilets, Angela (tour of duty she does every lunchtime to prevent bullying, she says), 'Isn't it good news about Andrew?' Could have murdered her. And she knew by word of mouth: no letter.

And then, to cap it all the Old Dear has *died* today. Again a mixture of feelings: at last the harassment can stop. On the other hand Benedict seems to be even more aggressive than usual: he actually followed me up the stairs (he often peers up my skirt when I go up anyway) and stood in front of the door to tell me. Is this how normal people behave? Perhaps this is how working-class people react to grief? Will he tear out his hair, gnash his teeth, burn all her belongings on a Viking-type pyre?

Feel uneasy being alone in the house with him. The old lady was some sort of limit on his insanity, a sort of rein. Now she is gone, what will he do?

I hope he doesn't *blame* me for anything. Even he is not *that* mad, is he?

7 *Electronics*

'He', Benedict, shut the diary on the last entry, and replaced it carefully, complete with the papers which were on top of it, in the back of the drawer.

He left the flat quietly, and walked down in the semi-dark to his own room.

Shaking slightly, unsure, he sat on the edge of the bed. Even at school he had not read so much, all at once. And such strange material.

*

Benny made himself a corned beef sandwich and a cup of tea. The quiet was extreme, as if the house were stewing beneath a tea-cosy. Standing by the door to the garden, Benny tried to think about Bet but found he could not. His mind was refurnished, polished. Only images of glass and polished wood and paragraph upon paragraph of small sloped handwriting crowded upon his eyes.

Benny brought cardboard boxes up from the cellar and filled them with Bet's clothes, bedding, magazines. Bet, bless her, had nothing of value. The photographs he carefully gathered together and took up to his own room.

He phoned Oxfam to come and collect the boxes, putting them out on the steps by the front door.

Bet had asked for this. All my little bits and pieces to Oxfam, won't you, Ben? An old Viking ceremony – the spoils to Oxfam.

Not stopping there, he dragged out her stained and crumpled mattress to the garden, together with her last bedding, pillows, etc., and with some paraffin from the cellar, set light to them. He tended the fire, adding to it from odd corners of her room, newspapers, old bags, some rotting shoes.

Only the Kiddy Alert and its wires did he spare, winding it up and unhooking the wire from the ceiling. He was going to need it. He had to search carefully for the drawing pins which had flown out all over the room as he pulled the wire from the ceiling. Popping like faraway gunshot.

Next door (on t'other side) Mrs Patel half drew her curtains as a mark of respect, as she had noticed Ben's curtains and Mrs Harrison had explained that the old lady had died in the night.

Also Mrs Patel did not wish her younger children to see the pyre which Mr Ashe was building to burn his mother. There seemed, she noted, peeping between her half-drawn curtains, to be no attendants, no relatives grieving with him. Should she go and stand with him and weep? She returned for a moment to the back of the kitchen and asked her elder daughter in Gujarati to keep the children away and to finish chopping the coriander leaves on the board.

Pulling the purple gauze over her nose and mouth, she drifted through her back door and down the path. She stood near her wall, looking at the pyre. She wrapped another layer of material about her face from her upper sari in order to keep floating soot from her nose.

Ben approached her, wondering if he should have offered her something before it all went to Oxfam.

'I am sorry about your mother,' said Mrs Patel, nodding towards the bonfire, 'she was a lovely lady.'

'Thank you,' said Ben.

'I didn't know you did this in England for a funeral,' she said, looking at the fire. Ben looked, and realised what she thought.

'That's not my mother, Mrs Patel, it's just her bedding, some of her belongings.'

'Oh, I see, and this helps you to grieve?'

'No, not really.' Ben thought, how can I grieve, show me how.

'It is a custom, then?'

Ben remembered burying the coins at Christmas-time and said, 'Yes, in a way. It goes back to the Vikings I believe.'

'If there is anything. Heavy things I can send my big son this evening, or if you need a hot meal,' she said.

Ben wanted her to hug him so that he could break down, but she was a stranger and he was a man, so he said if he needed any help he would come and ask for it.

Inside the house, working up a sweat now, Benny emptied the room entirely, moving everything either into the sitting-room in the front of the house (already a furniture store of a sort), or into his own, if precious or useful. Once empty he swept, Hoovered, and pulled these curtains down. A signal to Mrs Harrison that she could inform everyone, could now spread the word. He would not have to inform anyone now. Within the hour Charlie would ring and offer a full military funeral.

Finished. He shut the door and locked it. He would try never to enter this room again.

Everything from the kitchen he would no longer need too: spout cups, hot-water bottles, medicine bottles and measuring spoons. All trace of Mother gone.

Except from the very core of him where she rested, intact, young, beautiful, glittering: as an ambition to give him courage.

*

49

A woman with a Bedford van came for the boxes. He showed her the front room. Anything you want? No, she said, only small things. You might get a penny or two for some of this stuff, she said. That piano is worth something.

Then Benny made his camp. He cleared his room of everything unnecessary, all posters, boyhood pennants never taken down (triangles of pale wall behind). He moved in the table Bet's television had rested on and a chair, for his 'desk' on which he put the pieces of the Kiddy Alert, an ancient reel-to-reel tape recorder, a pair of headphones and some tools.

He also set up the television in one corner.

He looked into his wardrobe and wished he had donated its contents to the lady with the van. Perhaps he could buy some clothes now? With what? Had Bet left a will? He hadn't *found* a will. But it wouldn't be here, would it?

By the time Margueritte came home Benny had taken the Kiddy Alert to pieces, discovering which small bits were essential and which simply clumsy casing. In his line of work he had come to regard modern machinery as mostly casing. Jumping up he left his room and started down the stairs towards her. He felt suddenly shy, knowing so much more about her than he should.

She faltered on the stairs and put her briefcase down.

She smiled. He was standing two steps down from her, close, and their heads were on a level.

Emboldened by this smile he said, 'The funeral is tomorrow morning. Crematorium, eleven o'clock.'

'Would you like me to come?'

'Yes, if you can get time off work.'

She laughed, 'Funerals and nervous breakdowns are the only things my Head will gladly give time off for.'

Benny didn't bother to look puzzled at this remark, which was the beginning of his self-elevation in her eyes from someone who could understand virtually nothing, to someone with whom educated short-cut talk could pass for communication.

Benny sat in his room, his heart beating. Why? Fear? His hands shook too, so that he could not continue with his electronics, and turned on the television. It was the end of children's television and a tear sprang involuntarily from his left eye. At that moment the doorbell rang tentatively and Benny found one of the Patel children, a boy of about seven, standing there with a dish with tin foil over it.

'My mama has made you a meal,' he said, offering it.

Ben took the dish and crooked his finger at the small boy, motioning him to come in down the hall. He found the jar and gave him two barley sticks, still wrapped.

'How many brothers and sisters do you have?' Ben asked him.

'Three.'

Ben found another two sticks and the child left, beaming.

Benedict sat on his bed, now moved to be directly under hers, and listened, in the gloom.

So he knew that she was coming downstairs before she knocked on his door.

She put down a heavy box, with a wire trailing from it, with some effort.

'I wondered if you could get rid of this for me?' she said. 'It's a microwave oven which I don't think is a good idea any more. You could sell it, or just give it away.'

Ben swallowed a mouthful of his curry and asked, 'Does it work?'

'Yes.'

'Thanks.'

She went to bed early, about ten o'clock, and had the television on for about twenty minutes.

Before falling asleep Benedict went over his mental list. Unlike Margueritte he sensed the danger in ever committing yourself to paper.

8 *The End of the Line*

The morning of the funeral Margueritte went to work dressed, he noted with satisfaction, entirely in black, giving Benedict sufficient time to install the redesigned Kiddy Alert. He decided on the middle area, near the Yucca plant, under the floorboard between it and the skirting board. He only needed to bore a small hole with the hand drill. He had thought long and hard about the placing of the receiver, and decided that it must be some distance from the hi-fi, the bedroom being too close to interference from the TV. Besides it was not pillow talk he was after.

He also just had time, before leaving, to turn on the radio softly, go downstairs, switch on the box of the Kiddy Alert and listen on the headphones to, ironically, *Morning Service*, perfectly audible a floor away, through two shut doors. He might need to turn up the volume to hear conversations in the kitchen.

A female voice was saying that forgiveness was divine.

Right, thought Benedict: He might forgive, but I won't.

Benedict put on his only suit. It was an odd one, he thought, which Sharon had taken him to buy this summer. It was a lightweight grey suit, double-breasted, linen. He only added a black band around the arm, the same one he had worn for his father's funeral many years before. The trousers were extremely baggy and gathered to the waist. He thought, looking into one of Margot's mirrors in her bedroom, that he looked like an over-tall newly married salesman from a 1940s film. He only required a felt hat.

He polished his black shoes with a sponge on a plastic canister device he found in her kitchen and combed his hair, far too long now and slightly streaked with grey, back from his face, and waited on the steps for the limousine.

He stood by the Triumph under the shade of an avenue of yews waiting for Margot to emerge.

She did everything deftly. She put the car in gear, wobbling the stick slightly to check it was fixed, she reached into her glove compartment, arching her thin straight back slightly. She turned up and saw him. Her face like a white moon surrounded by clouds of blue-black hair tinged with henna in drifts from her hairline caught with a griffin hair-brooch at the back. She pivoted her thin white legs, together, over the leather edge of the seat and out of the door. Ben did not bend to assist her. She stood, locking the car.

'What a nice suit,' she said. Was she taking the piss?

'Australian,' he said.

Walking down the drive to the crematorium she walked so

52

slowly. She was wearing the impossibly high black patent stilettos. He quickened his pace and entered the crematorium without her.

Inside, seated in forlornly gappy rows, were Mrs Harrison, four neighbours Ben hardly knew, other than by sight, obviously women who never missed a funeral, Charlie and the three troops. Margot sat next to Ben in the front row. He was annoyed about this. Presumably she didn't realise the front was for family only?

Neither Charlie nor Ben's workmates nor Mrs Harrison looked Ben directly in the eyes. It just wouldn't be right. A person has the right to remain sealed on such occasions, private. Neither did Ben look at anyone, he merely took in who they were by the outline of their shapes sitting on the wooden benches while he walked to the front, peripherally.

But Margot looked around her at the collection of people with a brazen disregard for this convention and was branded instantly by Mrs Harrison and her cronies as a Hussy of the First Order. Ben only smiled.

Benedict did not kneel or pray during the short service, but Margueritte did. Was she asking for forgiveness, and being granted it?

The coffin slid through the curtains and disappeared, a few words more by the man in the long coat and they were walking back out into the dull day, a slight rain just beginning and Benedict felt an overwhelming sense of the wrongness of it all. It was all utter crap. Every word of it. He shook hands with everyone, all of whom could finally look him in the eye.

Charlie, dressed in uniform for the occasion, took Ben to one side.

'Well your dear mother is in the hands of the Almighty now, and we must look to the future.'

'Rubbish,' said Ben.

'One day you will see it, Ben. Wisdom comes with age, let me assure you. The line of command does not stop with us. No man is in authority over the whole world. Only Him, the Almighty.'

'You really believe that, Charlie?'

'Of course I do. Stands to reason. Her time had come. No one is to blame. Every soldier knows that.'

53

'You mean, if a bomb has your name on it?'

'Or a bullet, or cold weather, or a virus. He moves in mysterious ways. Not for us to question His commands. One day, Ben, one day.'

'Every day's another day,' quoted Benny.

'That's right, son. Anything you need, apply to me.'

He found Margot standing by him.

'Want a lift home?' she said.

Ben ignored the question and walked her to her car.

'Do you believe in all that?' Benedict asked her, just before she got back into her car.

'That's difficult. It's so complicated.'

'Do you believe, or don't you, that's all I'm asking.'

'Some of the arguments for the existence of God convince me, but my experience doesn't convince me that a benevolent, omnipotent being is *in charge*,' she said. That ought to shut him up. You can judge a man's worth by two things, her father had once told her: whether he has any friends of more than ten years' standing and whether he avoids talking religion.

Benny, a man with some friends of thirty years' standing (a fact which Margueritte was never to find out) was not shut up.

'All in all, then, no?'

'Overall, I suppose not.'

Good, thought Benny, very good. All the better. And it also crossed his mind that a woman who couldn't answer a simple question must be a lousy teacher too.

9 *First Forays*

Mrs Elizabeth Ashe had left her entire estate to her son, Benedict Ashe, the same comprising four hundred pounds in a Building Society savings account, and two hundred and twenty-five shares in an Australian uranium mine. The money Benedict swiftly removed from the Building Society, together with interest, and the share certificates he asked to be sent to Sharon's address. The funeral was paid for by the Co-op, a fact which would have amazed Margot who thought of them as a third-rate food shop.

*

Benedict was busy. Kept busy. Sharon phoned him twice that week. Did he need money? Would he come to them? How was he managing? Don't rush me Sharon, I've lots to do.

First he sold the microwave for two hundred pounds and *forced* Margot to take half the money, which she did reluctantly, saying that she did have a debt with the Inland Revenue. Benny resisted saying, 'Oh, not one of those Floating Whales, is it?' which would have meant his shooting up the scale of her admiration about two thousand points. There would be time enough for all that later.

Ben tried to join the library for the first time that week. They needed to have the recommendation of a member of the professional classes who had known him for two years. Only the doctor seemed to fit the bill and he was the last person Ben wanted to see. Neither did he want Ms Mason, teacher, who had known him for more than two years, to ask him why he suddenly desired to join the library. Ben decided he would have to borrow a card from someone else.

'Do you belong to the library?' he asked Charlie at the pub one night.

'No, but the library belongs to me, since I pay my taxes.' The other three people at their table laughed. 'Well, some of my taxes. I do make a contribution.' Charlie thought his Mrs had a card and Ben realised it had to be a man's card only, since he could not masquerade as a Mrs.

He gave up the attempt to join the library after two days, and decided to become instead a regular borrower at Margot's library, which meant he had to learn how to shift all the other books on a shelf so that there was no gap, but this had the advantage that he was reading the books she had actually read, assuming that she had read her own library.

'What d'you want to read, Professor?'

'Books, Charlie, just books!'

'At your age! What d'you want I haven't on video?'

Benedict was only thirty-eight in fact, though he had seemed fifty to Margueritte. By the time he had revolutionised his wardrobe, bought jeans with button-down fronts, shirts with wide green stripes and little white collars, an almost tweed jacket, grey shoes with a pattern of holes on the top, boxer shorts, and a jogging suit, and had his hair cut at a Unisex salon, he could have passed for a tall and slender twenty-nine-year-old.

Benny laughed at himself in the mirror. What a hoot! What do you look like, Benny, his mother would have said. I am trying to become Margaret Thacher's idea of a Youngish Briton, he might have quipped. No more quipping nowadays.

Charlie, using his vast knowledge of human psychology gained from a mixture of Falklands experience and his wife's women's magazines' problem pages, thought it best to inundate Ben with work. Take his mind off things. Ben was reluctant, of course (Charlie had expected this), and no doubt wished to wallow in self-pity, grief etc. Charlie knew better and sent him on dozens of little campaigns, mostly involving water down the set.

People will put potted plants on top of the set. They actually say, in plant shops, 'That'll look nice on the telly, won't it?' Why aren't the programmes enough? Or cactus, never watered? Inevitably there comes the day when they water the said plant overenthusiastically and some water spills down the open grids at the back. The picture fizzles, wavers, and disappears. All they need to do is open the back with a small screwdriver and blast the circuits with a hairdrier, but Charlie doesn't make this knowledge public because it provides his troops with much needed lucrative work which is straightforward. The sort of thing a man who has just lost his mother can do with his eyes shut.

'A hairdrier? Suzanne, get yours down will you?'

The fifteen-year-old in question has no intention of moving. She is hunched over the table at the far end of the room, her moussed hair flickering up and down, a style which resembles a winged creature just coming in to land.

'Suzanne! I won't ask you again.'

'Good,' she says, underlining something in her notebook with a transparent ruler, and sucks her pencil.

'You'll poison thysel' with that.'

'Good.'

The woman smiles at Ben and goes up for the hairdrier. He stands near the girl, between the fireplace and the television, its back on the floor.

'What you studying?' he asks.

'English,' she says. A man, her father perhaps, comes in the back door and puts down his snap tin, hangs his coat over a chair. He comes into the room. He exchanges some words with Ben who makes light of the silliness of watering a plant on top of a set. Then he informs him that his daughter is studying for her O Levels. Ben makes it clear that he is impressed and turns down the offer of a cup of tea.

Screwing the set back together, and making it work, Ben suggests gently that the plant be moved somewhere else. Another ornament could be put on top of the set. The mother looks round the room. There is a donkey with two paniers over its back. She replaces the plant with that.

Suzanne guffaws, 'Oh, God. Please, Mum, not that!'

The father starts to say something to her but stops himself. 'What d'we owe you?'

Ben rooted for change, and stood by Suzanne, trying to frame a question. The father looked puzzled, stayed put. Finally Ben said, to the downturned hairdo, 'Could you tell me what film or book Heathcliff is in?'

She looked up at him. 'Is it a joke?'

'No, I just wondered.'

'You're kidding. You don't *know*?'

Now the father seemed to come to life. 'Just answer him, my young lady. You who are so clever, now do you know or don't you?' He seemed to threaten her with untold violence if she did not say immediately. Ben wished he had not asked. Had not got her into trouble. He had a sinking feeling that she was going to say the Bible or something really obvious like that.

'Why should I?'

Oh, God, why doesn't she just say it?

The father swung at her and clipped her on the ear. She cried out and stood up. Ben tried to stop him saying it was all right, it didn't matter . . .

'It bloody well does matter. It's the principle of the thing. The girl has no *respect*.'

She was out in the hall, running for the stairs and shouted over her shoulder, '*Wuthering Fucking Heights* by Emily Fucking Brontë!'

Ben escaped before the father, shouting Just You Wait, could make it up the stairs after her.

Benny hired, after trying eight different video hire shops, a copy of *Wuthering Heights*, starring Olivier. He watched it during the day in the flat. He did not need to use *her* video, for he had rigged up his own, but he wanted to watch it in the right environment, imagining that he was *her*.

He fast-forwarded to the parts with Heathcliff in. The story did not interest him. It seemed to him to be like that old Yorkshire joke about a man standing on a bridge at midnight whose friend asks him to tell a story so he says there were two men standing on a bridge at midnight and one said, 'Tell me a story,' and he said . . .

Heathcliff. Seemed like your typical Sheffield lad, really – unemployed, loafing about with girls on the moors, unreliable (goes off for a few years, probably the merchant navy, for a few funds), quick-tempered, depressive.

Only for some unaccountable reason the actor speaks all those thees and thas with a public schoolboy voice!

Had Benedict known there was a book of the same title, he might have read it. It was sitting a few yards from him on the bookshelf. On the other hand, he might not, for he had never read a novel in his life, and was not *quite* ready to start.

Benedict stood to remove the video and saw in the mirror in front him, his back. This was a trick of the angles of the mirrors which Marqueritte had not forseen when she had them installed. Benedict had never seen his back, entirely. Glimpses of it in shops only. He stopped!

He straightened himself out, and ran his hand through his hair like Heathcliff did in the film. And laughed. It was hollow laughter.

Part Two

10 *Tactics*

A mere ten more days for the nation to transfer its assets to the coffers of the multi-million-dollar clothing and supermarket businesses: only ten more shopping days till Christmas and Margueritte, her annual improvidence successfully over, staggers up the last few steps with her bags all in one hand and opens the door to her flat with the other.

It is ten o'clock at night and she has just returned from a Saturday in Nottingham visiting the shops Sheffield has not yet heard of. Bags down, shoes off, she collapses on to the sofa. In front of her on the glass table top is a vase (her vase) full of yellow roses.

'What?' she said, out loud, to the room.

Someone had been in her flat. And left flowers. Only one other person had the key.

Her shoes hardly fitted now, since her feet had gratefully swollen in the few minutes since she had been out of them.

Ouch.

She knocked on his door.

'Come!' He was sitting on his bed, with Walkman earphones around his neck, and a book on his lap. What on earth could he be reading? Surely not a novel?

'You've been in my flat.'

'How did you guess?' He smiled at her. He looked different. Was this really Mad Benedict? He had had his hair cut, or, something. What? She gazed at him: he had suddenly become a gaze-at person. Especially since she hadn't seen him for weeks.

'You can't enter my flat without my permission. You know that.'

'I only wanted to give you the roses. They're from the garden. The last bloom of the bush.' Actually they were from Mrs Patel's garden. One of her children was allergic, so she had sent them round.

She shuffled around, her feet screaming for hot water.

'Oh. Thank you. But . . .'

He got up off the bed, hooking the earphones around the bedhead. 'They are to say sorry.'

'Sorry?'

'I think we can bury the hatchet now, can't we?'

'I never had a hatchet. I mean . . .' Her feet. She felt at a loss for words. What on earth did he mean?

'Now that I'm on my own, especially, I would appreciate the company, if you know what I mean?'

'No.' She involuntarily took one foot out of her shoe, for a moment's relief.

'Your feet are bleeding,' he said, 'such silly shoes!'

How did this happen? Benedict was in her flat, they were on the pink sofa, which seemed, for the first time, now that he was here, obscenely pink. Outrageously pink. She had her feet in a bowl of warm water and he was pouring salt into it. Bathing her feet, so gently, so gently.

Her stockings lay beside her on the pinkness, slightly blood-stained on the reinforced toe.

'That's fine. Thank you so much. That's . . .' he moved the sponge up and down her arch, around the ankle, a few inches up the calf, at the back. He wasn't kneeling, but squatting, like primitive people do.

'Just relax,' he said.

Exactly, he is not going to murder me, is he? I misjudged him. Up and down and round. He was just like an animal. Up and round. Not malevolent, just protective of his mother. That's only natural. Up and up. Me, he saw, wrongly, as the threat. Down, up, around. That is all over now. Now he feels sorry for me. Up and up. And God knows I need someone to pity me now that Dorothea is sending notes telling us what she will do after Christmas, what re-thinks she has re-thunk, and how we will have to shape up. Stroke, stroke. So if he wants to protect me, to care for me, stroke me, my poor feet, my calves, my knees . . . Knees!

'Benedict, my knees are okay!'

'Take all the impact, knees. Shock absorbers,' he was laughing, pushing against her hands on the knees.

*

She had to offer him a drink. It was the civilised thing to do, even at eleven o'clock at night. He asked her whether she had any Bruce Springsteen and, surprised and pleased, she asked him if he knew how to work the hi-fi. He did, and put the record on. Strange how men were programmed genetically to work hi-fi systems which women had to read twenty pages of manual to master.

They sat on either end of the sofa and drank wine and listened. It doesn't do to listen to the words of
I want a lover
to come on in
and cover me!
It doesn't do. He asked her what she had bought in Nottingham. How do you know I went to Nottingham, she asked. I know everything, he said. She giggled. How? I am psychic. Are you really? Yes. What did I get my mother, then? Let me hold your foot and I shall be able to tell you. OK.

A foot is just a foot. A faraway neutral piece of the anatomy.

She swung her faraway feet up to his lap and he stroked them there.

'A travelling alarm clock.' he said.

'That's remarkable.'

'Am I right?'

'No. But that's what I was going to get her. That's what I'd planned.' – And, incidentally, listed in the back of the diary.

'There you are then.'

The next day was Sunday so Benedict could not visit the flat during her absence. He would have liked to read the entry for last night, if she made one. To know whether his sudden departure had been welcome, distressing, or had inflamed her curiosity. He had thought it best to disappear a little mysteriously, like Heathcliff on the moors.

He had of course tuned in to her, and heard her having a shower and sitting down to the desk (everything scraped so nicely on the wooden floor) so she may have been writing in the diary, or not. These days she marked tests every evening and never went out. She worked *all* the time. Benny could almost find it in his heart to pity her for that. Almost.

*

That morning Margot saw, through the twigs of the limes in the weak sunshine, Benny fixing the front gate. He never looked up. He whistled while he worked. He was whistling the Bruce Springsteen song.

A few minutes later he strapped a large bag of laundry to the back of his bike and rode off, again not looking up.

The laundromat was full of people Benny half knew. Just to say hello to and remark about the fine weather. This is the Indian Summer: don't blink or you'll miss it. I won't.

Ben left his wash and rode off two streets away to see to a television. A retired couple who showed him their pigeons and their silver cups and gave him a mug of tea and a Lyons fairy cake.

Sheffield at its best: sparkling and clear and wonderful. Sunday was a long, long day. It rained. Margueritte wrapped her presents and addressed some of them. Margueritte was not here by mistake – it had been a political move applying for jobs in the Labour-run boroughs, where if the comprehensive system was not flourishing at least it was believed in. In other words she was still rebelling – against her quiet suburban upbringing in the tripartite conurbation, as the bald geography teacher might have called it, of Bournemouth, Poole and Christchurch.

Benedict went back to the laundromat, gathered up his clothes, cycled home, finished reading a science fiction novel, occasionally tuning in to Margueritte's operatic music. Sharon phoned, as she often did on Sunday, and had nothing to report except that Ronald was investigating the shares with great interest.

Margot watered all her plants with rainwater from the butt on the balcony. She tried phoning Andrew but there was no answer, as usual. She knew he would be round at Angela's but did not phone him there. Angela was pale and ill-looking these days and said that Sally's baby was teething and cried all night and slept only during the day, so she was not going to wake it up by phoning. She sat down to her pre-roasted songbird and asparagus at three o'clock, just after Benedict had eaten three pork sausages with beans and a small custard tart.

*

If only I had some excuse to go downstairs, thought Margot. But why do I want to? Just to see what he's doing. I don't care what he's doing; I don't. A little curiosity is only natural. He is a moron. A psychic moron perhaps? No, let him mend gates and do laundry and keep out of my way. But if I do run into him . . .

Benedict was waiting. He would wait until nightfall. Come the night and he would move. Like a nocturnal animal, Margueritte would have thought.

Night fell and it fell colder than it had done for weeks. The Indian Summer had left the dip between the hills of Sheffield. Leaves which had drifted up the lane amused at the householders' attempts to sweep them into piles now froze solid to the serious ground in the night frost, penitent and individual.

Benedict climbs one flight upwards, up her stairs. There is no need to use the key he has brought, the door is unlocked.

He had practised finding his way about in the flat with his eyes closed, so the darkness of the flat now presented no impediment. By sensation of touch alone he found his way to her bed, where she, naked between the silk sheets, opened her arms, and so on, to him.

Benedict had not expected to find the sheets so cold, or her so warm, but in no other way was he surprised.

11 *The Fifth Column*

During the days which followed before Margot was to leave to spend Christmas with her mother, there occurred a sort of retrospective courtship.

At first Margot was deeply puzzled – generally she had found that the men she had relationships with (which was a way of dignifying even brief lustful encounters) were extremely curious to know all about her, and she about them. In fact to Margot the only really fascinating thing left in adult life was Discovering

Other People. Such is the universal, middle-class, mid-life hobby: DOP. The fact that she had lived under the same roof as Benny for four years (off and on) did not diminish *her* curiosity about him. She watched closely to see how he shaved, how he tackled toast, how he laced his trainers, and most of all, what he said. She 'dopped' him closely.

But Benny seemed to have no curiosity about her. He did not even examine the flat very carefully (and after all it was his – you'd think he'd want to know). He listened to her talk (and how she talked, more and more as the days went by) but only with half his concentration, she felt, as if he knew it already. Because he spoke so little, so very little, what he did say took on a disproportionate significance.

Thus hourly Margot went over the small amount of information she had on him (all of it most surprising): he had not attended the school she taught at, but had been to the now demolished grammar school; his father, who had risen up through the Water Board, had died when he was only fourteen, and he and his sister had worked to support his mother, who had been an accompanist for singers, some of them well known.

That was all.

There were such gaps and inconsistencies in what little he told her that had it been a sixth form writing assignment she would have queried the feasibility, the plot. But she was not in a position, emotionally, to query anything.

He had friends, she could tell. When they walked the length of Psalter Lane into town, several people nodded to him or mumbled a greeting, and all eyed her most curiously. She had the uneasy feeling that Benny belonged to some subset of men (like the Masons perhaps) who did not talk in front of women, but about them, to each other, afterwards.

But this was unfair. He always answered a direct question squarely – he was not trying to deceive her, and she often reminded herself that his cultural and educational background was so different from hers that he could perhaps not articulate what he felt. But the disturbing fact remained that the sum total of the answers to her questions did not amount to the frank and fluent biography she was giving him.

For example, for some unaccountable reason (Benny could not account for it at any rate) she felt the need to tell him about

66

all her previous sexual encounters, each and every one, in some detail. Benny listened, with growing amusement (was he to believe this?) even when she was tearful over some rejection or disaster or other, and at the end of it (for they had arrived at one December night when her landlord snuck in the (unlocked, Benny advanced) door of her flat . . .) Benny merely said, 'I may be th'ony man you know who might *not* have AIDS.'

That sobered her for a moment. She nearly told him about Andrew and the test, but decided against. In fact she had changed most of the names in her summary.

'Why, haven't you . . . ?'

'Not lately,' he smiled, and moved away, out to the balcony.

Margot imagined he was dwelling on some simple young girl who had not waited for him, who had broken his heart. Someone who now had five children and lived in a council flat. He works by instinct, she thought, like those men of his class, simple, wise. She envied him that peace of mind which must come to people who do not intellectualise all the time.

Benny was in fact dwelling on the entry in her diary which he had read while she was at work, and congratulating himself on the 9 out of 10. Also, ruefully, he was wondering what would constitute a 10. And whether there was any way he could ask her this.

He turned back to her. 'Who was the best then?' He smiled at her.

'Best?' Why must men always be so competitive, what did he mean, exactly? Ah, he was probably thinking of the One and Only, the one who had deserted him early on. No one like that existed for her, so she gave him the romantic answer she thought he was seeking.

'You as a matter of fact.'

Then no one had scored ten yet? Thus Benny set himself a goal which he did not put into words, as a sort of corollary to his central plan.

It was Friday night. Tomorrow morning Margot was leaving for Bournemouth to spend Christmas with her mother.

'Will you miss me?' Margot asked.

'No.'

'Oh, thanks a lot.'
'I shall be working.'
'What at?'
'This 'n' that.'
'Shall I phone you?'
'What for?'

Benny felt restless. He walked around the flat, now dark, and switched on the tulip lamp, without looking for the switch. It had taken Margot a day to work out how it switched on. To Ben this lamp represented the logical and absurd conclusion of his theory that modern devices were almost entirely casing.

'Let's go out for a drink,' he said suddenly, 'to celebrate.'

'Celebrate what?' Now Margot felt it was her turn to be taciturn.

She stood, and was framed by the street lights' orange back-lighting from the french windows. This sentimental glow was achieved by virtue of the fact that this part of Sheffield used methane gas from the sewage below to illuminate the streets above – a scheme first suggested to the Authorities by Ben's father, and laughed at then. Benny walked towards her and put his arms around her, quite tightly, and kissed her.

'Being alive. Not everyone has that honour.' She didn't know whether it was a joke or not, since she had not fathomed him at all.

'Yes, let's celebrate that.'

Ben walked into the King's Arms briskly, with Margot behind him, as if she was an adjunct to him. She had seldom felt so confused. She nearly tripped over a placard in the entrance hall with 'Live Tonight – the Round Bananas' but Ben only glanced briefly to see whether she had fallen.

The Round Bananas were two black girls and a white man on a computer, and their noise penetrated all but the back bar. Benny led her through a door into the back, where a group signalled him to join them.

Ben did not introduce her, and after a while she realised he was not going to. The whole idea of introductions was stupid anyway, no one ever remembered your name, and it was just foolish Victorian manners, not real. So she made so bold as to venture a few down-to-earth remarks to a 'real' man on her right who seemed to know Ben rather well.

'Benedict seems to know a lot about televisions.'

'Ah, he would do – been known to make a toaster receive a picture.'

Someone said a piece of what sounded like a limerick, though Margot could not get the drift which was a shame because she liked limericks and knew a lot herself; she had often used them to interest low ability children in writing their own poetry. They all laughed. Margot laughed too, for the sake of politeness she told herself.

A man further round the table, next to Ben, asked him whether Margot's vest was a series of holes strung together with string, or a fishing net which had been the subject of an attack by moths. Ben smiled, but did not answer.

Margot felt the need to 'be brave' and keep back tears. Tears!

That vest reminded the man opposite of one which his dad used to wear once until his mother got rid of it.

Margot had been involved in too many exchanges with teen-age boys trying to prove something to get involved with this one. She knew that in the end the only thing she would not regret would be to keep absolutely quiet.

Margot did not so much wish she had not worn the vest, as that she had not been born. From time to time during the torture, from which Ben did nothing to protect her, she looked up at him and though a part of her wanted to kill him, or worse, a burning love took hold. She saw his face in profile for the first time and studied it and thought it to be the most perfect profile she had ever seen.

Oh, Ben, deliver me, she thought, over and over again.

After two and a half years and seventeen thousand rounds of drinks, during which Margot simply swilled back dry white wine as if it were water (it had no effect whatsoever), Benny got up to leave. On cue, Margot rose. There had been no 'ready, dear?', no 'shall we be making a move then?', simply the action, proprieto-rial, of standing up opposite her. She could no more stay sitting than she could have spoken Greek. So she stood. Her blood

69

joined her several seconds later, and the chair behind her fainted to the floor.

Now she had made a mess. Trust a woman to make a mess. Was she going to bend down and pick it up? He and his mates always advised young ladies to bend down most carefully in public places, for you never knew what stray hand might . . . not to mention eyes . . .

Margot tried to run out of the pub but there was a door in the way, which Benedict obligingly held open for her.

They walked back down a steep hill which had materialised while they had been in the pub. Also it was raining under Margot's fringe. She wanted to know whether those awful men were what you would call friends. Ben wanted to know – mind out, that's a wall – what else he should call them? She suggested some things he might call them and he expressed surprise that a young teacher should know those sort of words. Perhaps he had misjudged her? He also advised her to take his arm up the steps since they were now home. No, she could manage very well, she was *not* drunk. She had never been drunk in her whole knife. Life. Well, if she was not drunk, he didn't know what other word to use for it, perhaps she could also suggest some for that.

'Disgusted! That's a good word.'

'Well, it's OK. It's an OK word. Not my *favourite* word.'

Margot had the distinct impression that she was with someone else, not Benny. But perhaps it was just the wine.

The stairs up to her flat had been electrified in her absence and were now escalators going the wrong way, which was so inconvenient that Benny had to guide her up. She tried to shake free from his 'help' which seemed if anything to be slowing down her progress, but his grip tightened.

'They were just having a bit of fun, Miss. Aren't people to have fun?'

'Not at the eggs, the eggs, expense of others, they aren't.'

At the expense of others. Something about the phrase stopped Benny in his tracks. For a moment he wanted to obey her orders, to let her go. He could. He could just let her fall, over and over, crashing to the linoleum at the bottom.

No – too easy, too easy and too meaningless. Weakness that would be, just weakness.

*

They had reached the top and Benny placed his hand on the door and it vanished.

'Did you think,' Benny swung her round to face him, 'did you think ordinary men were like that Heathcliff, or that gamekeeper in *Lady Chatterley's Lover*? Did you think they were all like that?' She tried to free herself, struggling, pulling towards the darkened bedroom.

'No, I . . .' And what was he saying? About books?

'What do you row abrout brooks?'

'Shall I tak down me breeches for ee and say sweet nothins and worship thee an . . . ?'

They were in the bedroom, more or less. Benny had her by both elbows now, which were stinging under his Chinese burn.

'Let go of me!' He let go suddenly and she fell onto the floor by her own bed, banging her head on the rail. She held on to some nearby air for support and found herself spinning.

'Who am I, Margueritte? Who am I?' He was squatting by her, shouting.

'Oh, go away, go away.'

'If you used your little brain for one minute, that highly educated little puddle of grey cells, for just one minute . . .' Benny stopped himself. He had nearly lost control. Why should he warn her, why sabotage his own plan? She didn't deserve it. He lifted her on to the bed by the armpits. She was crying.

Ben's first thought was to unravel the string vest. It was a desire almost stronger than the other one.

He resisted the impulse and removed it instead.

Though she struggled while he undressed her, and though she repeatedly asked him to go away, her voice and her windmill arms lost their urgency gradually and her tears became beads of sweat.

Margot was aware, though inebriated, that something was going on which had gone on before, only more so. She was *reminded* of something.

'What's this going on?' she asked, panting. Her eyes would not come to rest on anything. First him then a triangle of dark mirror, then bedspread, then an arm jetting across the window.

'A. good. old. fashioned. fuck. is. what. with. no. twiddly. bits. just. like. in. the. books.'

'Could you say that more continnyously?'

He couldn't. Not just then.

When Benny left a few seconds later she was curled into a foetal position, saying nothing, like the back to front time-lapse re-budding of a rose.

He picked up the string vest lying on the floor and laid it over her pink legs, not at all tenderly.

12 *Retreat*

Margot woke alone. Alone except for the juggernauts revving up on her balcony, the string vest tearing into her flesh, and the hyperactive ceiling which was trampolining on her forehead. She showered under a deafening Niagara, drank several cups of coffee strong enough to tar roads, dressed, dragged her real leather suitcase over the three acres of carpet to the door, took her diary out of the desk, put it into her handbag, and left to catch her train.

On her way down she passed Benny's door. She made a point of not going in or knocking, but left the house, alone.

Alone in some ways, that is. Much baggage do we carry always with us: our memories, our conditioning, our genetic inheritance, small creatures fungal and bacterial which inhabit our hair follicles, our skin cells and the intricate ropes of our intestinal tract. Alone?

Even the tremendous force of Margot's electric shower nozzle's three-minute burst was not sufficient to dislodge those foreign bodies introduced into her body by Ben which may already have breached various natural defences (for there was not time nor opportunity to install the unnatural one habitually there) and might already be well on their way to egg-penetration, cell-division and all the rest of their one-act performance. Unlike Margot herself they would have no way of knowing it was the wrong time of the cycle for success, and her confidence would have surprised them.

*

Margot felt weak but not vulnerable. She could cope with anything. After all she had had disastrous affairs before. She was even now making a protest by leaving as planned, alone (except for . . .) and without so much as a goodbye.

13 *Northern Christmas*

Early Christmas morning over Sheffield, white with the first snow, and hundreds of thousands of glittering wire shapes on each roof, by the not yet smoking chimneys, sparkle and catch the first light of the sun, weak and orange. Only gritting lorries are out on the empty roads, a lone police patrol follows a stray dog down Sharrow Lane and a crow sits in the dead shopping precinct, nibbling at an empty crisp packet frozen to the pavement.

The good people of Sheffield do not need a visitation from Christ on this December morning, nor do they need choral services all up and down the Ecclesall Road (Episcopalian, Methodist, Roman Catholic, Chapel); they do not need the milkman who is having his one day's annual leave, nor the baker, for those of them who have no freezers have simply put food outside the back door under the steps to preserve it, and those who can afford neither turkeys nor extra bread are booked into the local church hall for a sumptuous meal. They do not need the shops along the precinct to open, nor the dentist (some of whom are in the South Seas in any case) nor the doctor, for the hospital will be open for real emergencies, for example for the victims of the inevitable domestic violence which will erupt on this day, with a skeleton staff entirely drunk. They do not need the services of an electrician or plumber or carpenter, for anything wrong with the house will now have to wait, and can wait, for it is the one day of the year when even the upwardly mobile couples agree to do no DIY.

But one thing they will need, on this day more than on any other day of the year – they will need Benedict Ashe. Should the television pack up on this, the day of the Great Watching, they will need a television-repair man and they will need him immediately.

Benny – Messiah, Saviour, Prophet of the Box, wakes at nine

73

and switches on his AirCall paging device. He dresses in a selection of the clothes he has abandoned recently in an attempt to impress Margot. But today Margot is not here; he is alone in his house. He has made no preparations for Christmas. None whatsoever. In a significantly different way to the bums and elderly penniless, Benny is relying on the community to provide for him all day.

Television sets went wrong all over Sheffield that day, and Benny attended each emergency in Charlie's distinctive van. The first at eleven o'clock in the morning.

Ben parked the van in the alley behind a row of small brick houses. He knew better than to knock on front and give them a nasty shock. Now that vicars stay put and social workers make appointments, it is only the police with warrants who use the front doorbell.

He walked straight into number twelve, with his bag of tools and his bag of spares, past a child playing on the small kitchen floor.

'He's here, Mum!' said a man of about sixty, talking to his wife, not mother.

The small front room was crowded with people – adults, teenagers, two small children and an elderly man by the coal fire with a pipe. Mum shushed many of them out, to give The Man some Elbow Room.

Not the old codger though, who watched him in silence.

Father squatted beside him as he took off the back of the machine, explaining what had happened. Ben nodded and started scanning the circuits. Simple job, ten minutes.

'Get the man a drink, Maeve,' said the Old One between clenched teeth.

'No, not to worry,' said Ben.

'You *will* have a drink.'

The smell of turkey and Christmas pudding was overwhelming. Ben would have liked something to eat, though it was early. Instead he smiled at the elderly tyrant sitting by the fire, no muscle of his face moving.

Mother brought him a small sherry in a proper crystal glass, and one for her husband and the old man.

Benny stood. The old man proposed a toast.

74

'To the Queen.'

Benny drank. To the Queen. Why not? He noticed that Father did not.

'To you, Dad, and a Merry Christmas.' He drank. The old man's faced moved now, for the first time. He took out the pipe and spat into the fire vehemently.

To Ben he said, 'He won't drink to his Queen, lad, what do you think of that?'

'Oh, don't you start, Dad,' said Maeve.

'On this holy day and her Head of the Church and he won't even raise his glass in honour . . .'

'Honour!' said Father, smiling sheepishly at Ben. 'He's a man who's fought for us in two world wars: more medals than I've had hot dinners and he wants me to drink to the richest woman in the world, who's done nowt for us and never will and whose corgis eat more food than I can give my kids. Parasitic bloodsuckers the lot of them. Come the revolution and I'll have a word to Royalty.'

The old man stood up (Ben had thought he couldn't) and advanced towards Ben, pointing with a yellow finger hewn out of ivory at the dawn of time.

'He drank to the Queen. He's not too good to drink to Royal blood.'

Ben backed off.

'Sorry, lad, take no notice,' said Father, 'and you sit yourself down, Dad, we don't want your legs going, do we?' Mention of the possibility of the departure of legs seemed to mollify him and he sat.

Ben replaced the back of the set and plugged it in. The picture wobbled, steadied, and he flicked through the channels. One channel was featuring the lady in dispute, so he turned quickly back to the Muppets which was no doubt what the children had been watching. The old man was seated again and the sound, now turned well up by Ben, attracted the children back into the room to sprawl out over the worn patch of carpet in front of it.

'Peace is restored,' said Father, beckoning him through to the back.

Out in the kitchen a small meal had been laid out by Maeve on a plate. A sandwich, pickled onion, and two mince pies. Ben sat and ate quietly. The mother sat opposite him, watching.

'Play darts at all, do you?'

'No. Fine game though.'

'Ay, fine game.'

Father offered him a ten pound note and two fives. Ben picked up the ten from the formica table and pocketed it. Later that day he was to charge six times as much for less work.

Using their phone, he called Charlie at home for the next address. Charlie wished him Seasonal Greetings and told him to come round for a drink the moment the going became lax. If it did. Meanwhile there was another call from just round the corner. It was indeed only two streets away, and again, he walked through the cobbles and into the back way. A neighbour was waiting for him by the kitchen door.

'She's on her own till the Sally Army comes for her, and she was crashing her stick on't wall so I came in and . . .' Ben went in to the next room. A tiny woman sat wrapped in old coats by the electric-bar fire in front of a dead television set.

Nothing wrong with the set at all. Ben turned to the old dear. The neighbour had gone home.

'How d'you usually turn it on, dear?'

She held up a remote control unit and waved it around in the air.

Ben had a look at it. Then he shook it. Something rattled. The crystal had come away from its casing.

Ben found one which worked in his spares bag. The cost of this unit was more than he felt he could ask for.

But he had to give it to her. He rang Charlie who asked him to make up the shortfall somewhere else. 'I have got to rely on your initiative here, lad,' he said, 'and I can.'

'Got any money, dear?' Ben asked, bending near her. She flinched. He felt like a mugger, as if he were threatening her.

'The sherry is in the sideboard,' she shouted, as if *he* were deaf.

'No, I don't want a drink.'

'You will not leave here on Christmas Day without having a drink,' she said. Ben sighed. When he went to the sideboard for a drink he found there a glass jar with five pound notes in it. Hundreds possibly. He poured two drinks, and gave her one.

'Can I take this?' he held up two five pound notes in front of her.

'Give me that,' she said and snatched it from him.

Leaving, Ben called in next door, through the window, and said he was going. A man came out, with an apron on and asked him to step inside for a drink. Ben couldn't refuse: the man had him by the shoulders. Sweet sherry again. Afterwards, the wife gave him ten pounds and said she would get it back – the old dear would suddenly remember and give it her.

Benny was fortunate to find himself in the British Legion at lunchtime, for he was starving hungry and having fixed the set on which they were all to watch the Queen's speech (only that) he sat down most gratefully in the kitchen with the staff and ate a full Christmas dinner, together with three glasses of white wine the chef considered too good for the guests, who were already The Worse for Drink – hadn't tha noticed?

Benny had. They gave him fifty pounds for tightening a few screws, and would *not* take it back.

Chef also insisted that Benny take home a box with half a turkey in it, about two dozen mince pies and some Christmas pud, to 'tide thee over' the next few days.

Thus fortified, and a little unsteady, Benny managed to find his way to Dore, an area of the town he would not otherwise normally frequent. It was the geographical place given to the subject of jokes in Ben's pub about rich people with no brains. Hence Ben assumed, without any proof, that it was entirely stocked with dim wealth.

A teenager answered the (front) door to him, and a dog nearly knocked him down.

'Are you the repair man?'

'I have come to see the television,' Benny heard himself say. There was no good reason to feel nervous, he realised, since this very teenager was probably taught by Margot.

'Fuck off will ya, I'm trying to listen to the stereo in any case, who wants the damn thing fixed?' She was about to fling shut the door when her mother came up behind, a woman with ample breasts and a flowing black velvet skirt underneath.

'Fiona. Go to your room and stay there. I am so sorry, please come this way.'

'This way' took half an hour. The hall itself was bigger than any private house Ben had entered that day. Benny followed, his bags swinging against his legs painfully, her velvet fulsomeness regal and pneumatic (ah, bliss therein) before him. Like a procession. The pot plants made Margot's look like dwarfs. Perhaps they were dwarfs? Who? Benny felt more and more unsteady, and the floor seemed *spongy*.

Bending forwards (oh those mounds, those mounds, fringed with lace daisies and a string of pearls aching to break and flow down the chasms between . . .) the woman opened an oak wardrobe at one end of the aeroplane hanger of a sitting-room and revealed a twenty-six-inch colour television.

'Oh, clever!' Benny said, before he could stop himself. He never would have guessed it was a television. Perhaps the whole wall behind it lined with books was really videos and drinks cabinets?

'Yes, I don't like the gogglebox to *seem* to be the focus of the room.'

'No, of course not.' Benny smiled widely. What should he do now? Open the white lace front of daisies to reveal – a forty-six-inch full colour set of . . .

'Neither sound nor picture. I hope it isn't the tube.'

'Oh I hope it isn't the tube,' Benny said.

'I'll just go and get you a drink. Is there anything else you'd like?'

'A drink would be wovely.'

Oh God, another drink?

The hardest part was getting the back off the wardrobe. It was a carpenter's job really. Fiona brought him a drink and giggled at him.

'I've sabotaged it,' she said, giving him a glass of whisky with ice in it.

'Tell me what you've done and you can have the drink,' Ben said. He was not without guile himself and couldn't bear the thought of tracing a fault with his now wobbly hands.

She considered this. Looked at the whisky.

She sipped at it and said 'ecstasy' and drank a whole gulp, gasping afterwards. 'Fuse in the plug. But make it last, or she'll know.'

78

While Fiona sat next to him sipping the drink, he put the machine back in its coffin and opened up the plug.

'Are you married?' Fiona asked him.

'No. I screw my lodger,' he said, giggling himself.

'Do you *really*? How exciting. Who is she?'

'Did I say *she*?'

'Oh, *really*? Even more exciting.'

Fiona was called away, gave him the glass, ran off, bumped into a piece of furniture the size of a desert cactus in Arizona, and disappeared. Benny explained to the Mounds that several multi-functional diodes had transpired and fused into circuit-breaking thermal nodulations and it would cost her sixty pounds, he feared. She was happy to pay him and explained that she did not watch it herself but had guests coming who would need to watch the Queen's speech, especially since one of them would be writing about it in next Sunday's paper.

He thanked her for the drink, being careful not to name it in case it had *not* been whisky.

Turning out of the drive, congratulating himself on handling the dim wealth with such panache, Benny caught sight of Fiona up in one of the bedroom windows. She was sitting, quietly like any fourteen-year-old, lonely, with earphones on. She waved to him. He didn't wave back. Between here and the next call, on the council estate, he could get enough strong coffee to sober up.

Benny drove around aimlessly for a while, looking for an Asian grocer who might provide him with some black coffee, almost getting lost, before he gave up, largely because it had started to snow.

The council estate's appearance was improved by the snow. All graffiti was automatically whitened, rusting and rotten window frames held sentimental triangular drifts of white, like chocolate-box windows, even the dusty shrubs failing to grow in concrete took on the aura of misshapen Christmas trees. The darkening sky too gave the whole place, street upon street of perpendicular or horizontal, of grand grid of roads and street names like Wesley Avenue and Churchill Drive, a Christmas card elegance.

*

The wind was getting up too by the time Benny found the place and knocked on the (side) door. A young man with two toddlers at his knees came to the door.

'Thank God you're here. It's the big Walt Disney any minute.'

Benny went in, took off his coat (the warmth was stifling), had a brief look at the new baby, in a pram in the hall, and went to the set. Absent-mindedly he drank the beer they gave him while he took the set to pieces. Both parents spent the entire time keeping both children away from these pieces. Puzzled, Benny reassembled the set.

They sat in silence, the dead screen grey and cold.

A knocking came from the ceiling, or beyond.

'What's that,' asked Benny, 'someone upstairs banging?'

Her face pale, the young woman bundled the children away into the hall and the man said, 'My wife thinks it's haunted. I've told her not to panic, but we've been getting this noise for nearly a week now.'

Benny stood and listened. He went with the man to the upstairs of the house. The banging was stronger.

'It's the aerial,' Benny said, wishing he had not drunk the last beer.

'What?'

'Your aerial is down and hanging by a thread so to speak, banging in the wind.'

'Oh, thank God.'

'What's thank God about it? We'll have to go up and mend it.'

'Yes, but at least it's not a ghost.'

Benny had deliberately said 'we' for he was not going up alone. A ladder took him to the edge of the roof, and the young woman stood holding it while her husband joined Benny aloft. The wind was like the wind on board the deck of a liner.

Benny laughed. 'What a view,' he said.

'I think I'm scared of heights. This high anyway.'

'No you are not. It's all in the mind. Like ghosts.' Benny laughed again.

'Please don't laugh. You might cause an avalanche.'

No, that's right, it's serious, trying to keep hold of these little bits of wood, these rods at intervals on the slate roof. The tiles

80

are none too firm either but even the firm ones were frozen and now covered with snow.

Ben cleared each area of snow before climbing to it. The aerial finally came into sight, hanging forward across the central section of the roof. The wire attached down beside the chimney was almost within reach.

It was inevitable that they should fall, one or both of them. Perhaps there was, in a way, some evil spirit abroad; or simply the action of the spirits on Benny.

It doesn't really matter whose foot missed, or whose hand clutched at the other man, or who said the Rude Word first or who dragged whom over the edge, down along the slope of the bicycle shed (thank God for it) and into the drift which had (mercifully) collected between the houses, for neither of them was in the least bit hurt, and their fall somehow wrenched the aerial back into a position in which it was happy to receive at least BBC. Never mind, said Benny, I don't do aerials really. You can get a man round when the holiday's over. The Queen is on all channels. She is a cross-channel Queen really.

He laughed.

The young wife laughed too, and then her husband laughed and the children started laughing and Benny thought he would become hysterical if it didn't stop soon.

'Would you like a drink now, a stiff drink?'

'Food is what I need.'

'Ah, Gill, make the man some turkey sandwiches will you?'

'Could I have anything but turkey, please? Even snow sandwich would be fine, or coal.'

'Or dib-dob,' yelled the children, joining in the fun, 'or wee-wee, or . . .'

Ben finally made it to Charlie's house now, for that drink. While he was there the Batphone, as Charlie's grandchildren had named it, rang. It was a closed-circuit job at a bank. At first Ben thought it was a joke (bank – Christmas Day?) but Charlie took him to one side and explained.

Ben enjoyed the drive across the moors now that the snow had stopped. Sheep huddled in groups near the road.

The Northland Bank's nuclear bomb-proof shelter came into view. Ben had never seen it before. Shallow twin domes rose out of the snow beyond a crude road-frontier barrier.

Ben was frisked and a security pass was pinned to his chest; his tools and spares bags were searched thoroughly, as was Charlie's van. Fortunately they did not breath-test him, for he would have failed miserably.

A section of the larger dome slid up and a man in grey uniform took him into a primitive lift cage. They descended for what seemed like minutes – reminding Ben of his one trip down a coal-mine shaft. Only it smelled of nothing rather than soot.

Underground was the mainframe computer. Ben toured the sets which were attached to swivelling cameras covering the whole subterranean installation. The fault was what Charlie had predicted. They offered him coffee, which he needed, twice. When the job was done he re-ascended, perplexed and frightened.

We could all die but our *money* would be safe. Our *money*! He stared at the barrier guard, who stared suspiciously back.

Margot phoned at midnight. Benny was asleep, fast asleep, when the phone rang. He did not answer it. He was on call for tomorrow also, and needed the rest.

14 *Southern Christmas*

'You don't have to take me the scenic route, Mother, I'm not a Grockle.' Her mother was missing gears along Overcliffe Drive, along by the blocks of exclusive flats with views of the Isle of Wight (on a good day, on tiptoe) and down towards the even more exclusive eight-bedroomed detached bungalows with shell gardens, only a dangerous walk away from the beach itself. In fact she had only come this route because it avoided roundabouts which meant she needed to be able to steer and change gear simultaneously which she had never mastered.

'I wish you wouldn't use that word, it's so ugly.'

'But I like to use the local words. I have to belong somewhere.'

'We like to call them Visitors now.'

*

We? Now? What has happened in her absence? Perhaps some dreadful virus has swept across the south coast and infected everyone with terminal niceness? Malignant tolerance; inoperable patience.

If it happened anywhere, it would be here. In the better climates and coastal regions of anywhere 'civilised' puritanism thrives. Capitalism comes up perfect and luscious like a new cutting of it potted in the very best compost and lovingly nurtured on the stripped-oak window-sill of prosperity. Success is as sweet as that smell after a good rain on rich soil, aromatic, upwardly mobile.

Margot's mother, in her crisp middle age, steers the car carefully into the garage. Even though Margot is here, she is in no hurry to enter the house, the car must be housed first, and the garage doors shut and locked. Especially, she tells Margot, since her nearest neighbours (a wedge of green baize and a small copse away to the left) are in Florida at a Dentists' Convention..

Margot's mother was elderly when she came. She has slid back into middle age. This is an occupational hazard of living here: people come to Bournemouth to die, and then change their minds, join the Conservative Party and start a small business.

Margot's mother had been to evening classes and then made corn dollies, mostly for charity sales. It had given her something to do in her widowhood.

What dawns on Margot during the next few hours, when in fact she most needs her mother to be open-minded, thoughtful, supportive, is that her mother has been infected with the illness that gathers in the wake of all this puritanism and capitalism. Too early widowed, without grandchildren to take away the sting, and too seldom in receipt of letters from Sheffield, she has taken a lover, and normally nothing would have pleased Margot more, only this is the lover who devours his mate: Jesus.

Margot had no way of knowing that fundamentalism had been sweeping Bournemouth, that in the recent General Election the inhabitants did not so much vote for Thatcher, as for Reagan. In primary schools up and down the coast (inland a healthy

83

scepticism is in its twilight sequence) teachers are being asked by seven-year-olds if the bible stories are actually *true* and being told that of course they are. Small girls walk home, heavy with the internal burden of Jesus. Jesus is in me, Mum, what is he doing in there? Will he burst out? Help!

It doesn't matter, Daddy, if this stick pokes my eye out, for Jesus can make the blind see. That's only a metaphor, son. No it's not, Daddy, it's *true*! PUT THAT STICK DOWN.

Even if she had guessed it, Margot would not have worried on her mother's account; surely her mother was a tough and independent-minded woman, and not to be swayed by a bunch of rebels and weirdos at her age.

Trouble is, they are no longer rebels and weirdos – they are the establishment itself, and even the strength of Margot's mother's mind is not adequate to defending itself against what seemed to be at first nothing more than a cheerful enthusiasm for Life. Lift up your Porsches and Ride! Yuppies Unite! Have you got time for Jesus – He's got time for you.

And all over Bournemouth in front windows, grand and not so grand (for there are no slums here, no terraces, only levels of wealth), the glass sports the wing-shaped blue and gold sticker with 'He's Here' etched across it in breathless italic.

Why?

Why is He here?

Margot files away the following story as she used to file away stories for Andrew, forgetting that Benedict would not be in the slightest bit interested though Andrew would have been fascinated. It nicely sums up, she thinks, why it is she is unable to communicate with her mother any more.

Her mother tells her of a new housing estate they are building near the sea, further down the coast. It will be the most prestigious place to live for miles. The houses are rumoured to be valued at about twice what it would cost you to live in a reasonably central part of London.

The first designs drawn up were for five-bedroomed houses with four reception rooms, triple garages, spacious gardens, and a *swimming pool*.

Since the houses were going to be so expensive, the building

84

firm did some market research to find out if these houses would be indeed the dream homes of people wealthy enough to afford them.

No. Surprisingly they were not. What was missing? Nothing – nobody wanted the swimming-pools. Why not? Heated, you could swim all year in this gentle climate of Bournemouth.

Margot's mother was puzzled – what did she think?

Margot saw it immediately – a return to the Old Values. Those old Hollywood films where a man strikes oil and he and his Gal settle in the twenty-roomed mansion. Their daughter wants a pony. She must have one, she must have everything she wants. One day she falls from the pony, over a jump, bangs her head and dies. All the money in the world does not console them for the loss of their daughter. Why did the gods take the child? Because no one deserves to be so rich. And we, the audience, are secretly pleased – why should they have everything, when we have to suffer?

So a lavish house with a swimming-pool is asking, just asking for Him to take your children from you, asking for them to be drowned.

See? Success is difficult for Christians, to whom guilt is as normal as daily bread. You can't give it all away, that wouldn't be sensible, but somehow you have to live on a knife edge, apologising to God all the time for the easy life you only hope will console you for the kids who don't love you, because you won't give them that pony, that swimming-pool . . .

'Oh, God. In whom I can't believe,' wails Margot silently to herself at dinner that Christmas Eve with her mother, where are all your lovely Jews? Why don't they put a stop to all this nonsense?

All Christmas Day Margot felt her mother was going through the motions for her sake. They circled round each other like two warlords equally armed, afraid to strike a blow by mistake. Gratefully Margot retired to read a book by half-past ten, and read long into the night. At midnight she tried and failed to phone Ben.

*

She was expecting to rise late on Boxing Day and finish her novel while still in bed, sipping luxuriantly on a cup of real coffee her mother had thoughtfully delivered. Then she had expected to wander downstairs to help prepare a few vegetables.

They would eat on their laps, there being no need for the dining-room now that Margot's father was no longer there to insist on it. They would watch the television and drink Beaujolais.

The afternoon would pass in a fug. She would fall asleep in the large armchair and doze for an hour or so. Then she would make her mother a cup of tea, cut her a piece of cake, chat idly about this and that. Possibly one of them would bring up the question of her latest liaison, the euphemism wide enough . . .

So she was surprised to find herself in the rain outside a modern church hall at half-past eleven on the Friday morning, being buffeted by seventy or so children all charging out of momentarily halted cars and into the double doors of the hall.

'Mother, what are we doing here?'

'I told you I help out here on Fridays.'

'But it's Boxing Day.'

'It's still Friday and every Friday we have the Pioneers.'

'What?'

The Pioneers were colonising their environment by means of riot inside the hall. Margot's mother seemed to think this was quite in order and took off her coat in the corner, hanging it on a peg and greeting a young man with an inane smile. This is my daughter who has come for Christmas, down from Sheffield. Oh, how wonderful, and is she with us in Jesus? No, not exactly. Not yet, you mean. The warmest of welcomes, Margot. Thank you. And God bless you.

God – don't you dare. Margot pulled her anorak about her, would have liked to pull her surname too. I am Ms Mason to you, she wanted to say to the fifteen-year-old, not Margot. This place was only one short prayer away from Bedlam itself.

To see her mother gazing about her, you would have thought it was the Dresden section of her favourite department store. Perhaps Jesus made you temporarily blind and deaf at the Pioneers?

*

Margot sat at the back of the hall, inspecting the teaching skills of a young man. The young man who leapt onto the stage and took up the stance by the microphone of a pop star about to thrill his fans, was Dave. He was young too, agelessly fanatical. Margot counted seventy-five children, their ages from five to nine, interspersed with about six adults, varying from teenagers to her mother in age. Everyone stood chaotically in groups. Some children, obviously unassigned as yet to groups, wandered between sets.

'Walk three times round the room!' bellowed Ayatollah Dave. Since he had omitted to say in what direction, a tidal wave of crashing infants erupted and Margot ran for cover.

The Ayatollah did not notice any of this for he then asked them to change direction and walk the other way. Everyone did so, even Margot's mother, and another tidal wave challenged the first for noise.

'Right, good,' said Dave, 'now shut up and get into groups.' The tidal wave collapsed, exhausted, and battered groups of five-year-olds sat down where they were and the older boys became aeroplanes and continued tidalling.

Dave threatened everyone with 'losing points' if they did not sit down in groups before he had finished counting to three.

'ONE, TWO . . .'

They sat. Except the new ones who wandered about since they had no groups allocated to them.

Dave then asked them to place a certain part of their body, e.g., the foot, on someone else's body, e.g. tummy. This gave the all-male groups near Margot at the back splendid opportunities for kneeing each other in the groin, kicking each other in the stomach, etc. One boy trod on another's face. Margot felt something rising inside her: the desire to shout, 'STOP THIS STOP THIS STOP THIS'.

But she didn't. She was outnumbered, and afraid.

Shaking, Margot joined them on the floor, where they had been ordered to sit for The Story. In *complete* silence. At last the violence was over and a sort of order was establishing itself, albeit an enforced one.

*

A young girl in jeans and sandals took the stage and adjusted the microphone. Behind her Dave and an associate placed a larger card on the stand – the Visual Aid. The visual aids were three cartoon drawings, silhouette-style, of two men in Arab dress and a woman with long hair.

Under the two men were the names 'Simon' and 'Jesus' and under the woman was 'Mary'.

Ah, but which Mary?

The story which followed was about prostitution and the Jewish touch-taboo. Margot was shocked – it was not a topic she would have cared to handle with fifteen-year-olds, but given that it was chosen, presumably with some care, why was it so badly done? Having said that Mary was a 'naughty' woman (you could hardly go into details), and that Simon was a Pharisee, the story did not explain why she washed Jesus' feet, but then dived off into Jesus's complex metaphor about the cancelling of a financial debt. This metaphor is a good one for adults, who understand about mortgages, but the teller of the story realised she could not explain it sufficiently for these children and so kept saying 'anyway' and carrying on. Anyway, by the end of the story the frowns on the little faces about Margot were almost as profound as Jesus' sentiments on forgiveness. The word 'forgiveness' was not used in the story, though this is a concept that children, who are constantly chastised and forgiven in their day-to-day lives as they do naughty things, would have readily understood. No mention in fact was made of what the story was about at all.

Never mind, thought Margot, now they can ask questions, like, 'Is that Mary the Mother of Jesus, and what does the story mean?' Wrong again. Margot had got it wrong, for then Dave leapt on to the stage like an avenging angel and shouted, 'This really happened! It's not just a story, it really, REALLY HAPPENED.'

Margot's mouth dropped open – surely even the writer of the gospel itself would dispute this; that the message is what's important not the historical accuracy. And in any case, what does the historical truth matter to children, isn't moral education the point?

Dave was suddenly on fire on the stage. 'What's PJN?'

Everyone in the room, bar Margot, shouted, in response, but

not in the manner of an ecclesiastical response, rather in the manner of a Hitler Youth Rally, 'PEOPLE   JESUS   NETS!'

'What's PJN?'

'PEOPLE   JESUS   NETS!'

'I CAN'T HEAR YOU!'

Margot fought the desire to vomit into the coat-stand. Is this England??

They were then given the choice between a 'quiet' and a 'noisy' game and split into two.

The noisy game consisted of the helpers chasing the children in ever-diminishing circles with frightening abandon. It looked like a rehearsal for football hooliganism.

Margot's mother had not prepared anything as she didn't know she was going to have to do this – i.e. the Quiet Thing.

Obviously in something of a dilemma, she initiated a game suitable for three-year-olds. She thought of an item you could buy in a supermarket and they had to guess what it might be. They were divided into two teams, though she did not define the competitive element, and no 'points', mercifully, were scored.

Then they split into Squadrons (the military reference was not lost on some of the older boys who zoomed about with out-stretched arms) for 'activities'. Dave had some difficulty settling those who had been running amok, so he was obliged to use the threat/points system to 'shut them up'. The 'activities', all except the last, were playgroup activities, the level being at least four to five years below most of the children: one group put already made-up liquid icing (with poisonous food colouring, very strong) in between two digestive biscuits; one group stuck pink tissue paper on to a card for a Valentine greeting – a strange idea, as it celebrates a pagan fertility festival, or is it a commercialisa-tion of lust? Another group coloured in posters advertising the Pioneers with felt-tips. The last group did Drama.

Margot – by profession a drama teacher – watched a totally unqualified boy (perhaps seventeen years old?) fail totally to do anything useful with a group of children who were bursting with potential.

First of all he had discipline problems which he had no idea how to solve. Two boys were being disruptive. He tried to force them to 'be Jesus', and failed. He received insults from them and

89

banished them to the top of a stack of chairs which they then swayed on dangerously. He did not settle the children, or explain to them what the story (the one they had heard) was about. When they complained that they didn't understand what to do, he simply shouted irritably that he would have to tell them what to do then, if they were so stupid that they had not understood it.

The 'play' they managed to come up with depicting, supposedly, the story of Simon and Mary, consisted of the group walking around, sitting on chairs and saying words, which he whispered to them, about five hundred gold coins. They 'performed' this play afterwards to the entire group, assembled in the hall. If anything, the story now seemed even more confusing.

Suddenly there was much leaping about onstage again as one of the helpers hoisted a board up with pie-charts of the squadrons and their respective 'points'. There had been no mention of how you gained points, but there then followed the most hideous and divisive bit of rabble-rousing outside a pantomime (where it is not in earnest, and therefore fun). The children had to cheer and boo according to who had the most points. And those who had the least points would have to try harder. Won't they? *Much* harder.

Dave then led all in the final prayer. The prayer said this:
    a: Thank you, God, for the Pioneers.
    b: Make all the sick people we know well.
    c: Give us all a nice weekend, God.
    d: Amen.

Is this right? Is it not a very short way from 'Give us a nice weekend, God,' to 'Give me a Hornby train set, God, with two carriages, like my friend has'? Is God as Magician the idea we most want to give our children?

Since Margot was not one of those who had dared to be talking while Dave was praying she did not have to stay behind to see him. She was glad of this. She hadn't suspected for one moment the Eternal Truth that God doesn't like it when people interrupt Dave when he is talking to Him. He doesn't like it *at all*, apparently.

90

And any resemblance between Dave's depiction of God and the Head of the Mafia is purely coincidental, thought Margot. Had her mother not been there she might have spoken to Dave on the topic of aya-tolerance.

'Mother, that was appalling. I have never seen such disgusting indoctrination, outside films about Hitler Jugend, in my entire life! How could you be a party to it?'

Her mother smiled. Did she turn the other cheek, just ever so slightly, ever so smugly?

'Dave warned me you would say that. Just because you are a trained teacher, Margot, there is no need to poke fun at those of us who are doing our best to instill the Holy Spirit in the young ones.'

'But the competitiveness, the violence, the mindless chanting of "People Jesus Nets", the – '

Her mother turned, on the verge of an unchristian anger for one moment, checked it, and said, 'I know you like to think of me making corn dollies for the CND and twiddling my thumbs at coffee mornings, waiting for a monthly letter from you, but you find it hard to accept that my life has Meaning.'

'Ah, it's my fault for not writing is it?'

'If that drove me to Jesus, then I thank you, Margot, from the bottom of my heart.'

Margot needed to be on her own. At times of emotional stress she always sought solitude. She sat in her room and wrote a poem, something she had not done since she was sixteen.

This is the poem:

To my Mother, now lost.

Beware the casual Jesus at the door
Asking for a pallet on the floor.

Casting no shadow, with empty sleeves,
He put on magic shows beneath the eaves
Revealing stars beyond your roof,
The grass below your floor. You never asked
For any other proof.

Beware the casual Jesus at the door
Asking for a pallet on the floor.

He was all this and Saviour too –
For ever now the pallet is for you.
In the broken chambers of your heart
Only the empty sound of grateful prayer
Now – echoes – there.

The poem did not really say what she meant, which had always
been the problem. The technical exigences of the form always
seduced her in the end. She had not the will-power to open the
door fully to her real feelings, the bitterness, the hatred.

Her family had always been a ritualistic one. No one ever said
what was on their minds. She felt sure that her father had died
without ever hearing the words 'I love you', and perhaps she
would too. Her mother on the other hand had found a group of
people who began every other sentence with 'I love you and God
does too'.

Seeing that England, the country in which both Margot and
Benny passed the Yuletide days, seems to have stretched itself
out like that sticky blue stuff you can hang posters with, until
the middle is one molecule thin and about to break, it is a
wonder really that you can make a simple phone call from one
end to the other, and a wonder that the language is so similar.

Somehow Ben's attack, if that's what it had been, had been at
least an expression of his black side; there was nothing hypocritical about it, nothing parsimonious, nothing self-satisfied, and
she soon found herself longing to hear from him, to have
evidence that the rest of the world was not simply a figment of
her over-active imagination.

'Hello, Ben?'
   'Yes, it's me.'
   'Hello.'
   'Who is that?'
   'Me, of course.' She heard shuffling in the distance, rustling
and a slight click.
   'Oh, Margot.'

92

'Two days and you have forgotten me!'
'I have not forgotten you. I was fast asleep.'
'What have you been doing?'
'Sleeping.'
'No, I mean all day.'
'Repairing televisions.'
'I have been . . . well . . . my mother is into Jesus. It's awful.'
'It's just the time of year. It's Christmas, Margot.'
'No, I mean all year round she is into Him. She is high on Jesus. She is born again.'
Ben chuckled softly. 'How nice for her.'
'You don't understand.'
'Can I go back to sleep now, Margot?'

Margot walked quietly up the deeply carpeted stairs, past her mother's room where she heard, faintly, through the slightly open door, the sound of urgent whispering.
She knew her mother was praying for her.

All night long Margot could hear unscheduled trains shifting harmless plutonium waste through the home counties, only in London they pronounce it 'armless'.

15 *Least Resistance*

You may have been thinking (I forgive you) that Andrew Furness is a complete scoundrel, without mitigating characteristics. Well he is not. Few men are. Or women. Even one-parent, black, sexually ambiguous ladies can make interesting companions, as Benny would be able to tell you later on this week.

Andrew knew that Margot was due to return from her mother's on the day after Boxing Day, the twenty-seventh, a Saturday. Apart from the fact that they often spent Saturdays together (or had done before the advent – oops, unfortunate seasonal slip of the mind – of Angela) Andrew felt that he could not let the Christmas school break go without seeing her. It would be downright cruel of him. He felt guilty on many scores – mostly to do with a fine sense of justice rather than any sentimental attachment to Christian ethics. Was it just, after all, to take Margot at her literal word about their independence when it most suited him, and at the same time expected her to be available for him when that suited him most? He was still sufficiently accustomed to confiding in her, despite Angela's colonisation of him, to feel that he would not like her to take up with someone else. In fact the very thought of it made him feel rather queasy.

Parking behind her car in the snow on Psalter Lane, which seemed unusually bright for once, he looked up to the top of the house to see if her blinds were drawn. They were half up. He had come to make a clean ... er ... breast of it, and for a pressing reason, and sat in the car going over possibilities.

Margot had come home that morning, fully resolved to put an end to all this nonsense. She had had plenty of time to think at home. In fact it was almost the only topic on which she could think without total despair while there.

She had not succeeded in telling her mother anything about Benny at all. Her mother's new-found generosity of spirit did not extend to wanting to know anything about her daughter's life whatsoever.

She had, that evening after the abortive telephone call with Benny, decided to call it off, and to look for another flat.

The best thing, she had decided, would be to take up Andrew's long-ago offer of moving in with him. At the time she had thought that he would become too possessive, they would sink into the morass of married coupledom, but now not only did that conventional situation look rather attractive compared to the mess she was currently in, but also she had worked out, in the vacuum of Bournemouth, that the whole business with Daft Angela was a test of her resolve – an attempt to get her to agree to cohabit. And now she was ready.

At least, for all his faults, Andrew was not fanatically anything, except possibly, tidy.

So the following morning she was almost surprised when Benny let himself into the flat just as she was having her first cup of coffee of the day, and sat down, as if he owned the place. Oh.

She handed him a cup of coffee, and sat down with hers. 'I have decided,' she said, 'that from now on we won't, you know, go to bed.' She gulped her coffee, looking into the brown puddle, not at him, it would somehow be fatal to look at him.

'I agree,' he said, brightly.

'What?'

'I agree. That bed of yours isn't a proper bed. It's just a slab of uncomfortable wadding over some slats. No springs. No give. Rigid. I never liked it.'

He was talking about her futon in this way! Sacrilege! 'I'm not talking about furniture, Ben.'

'I thought we were.'

'Don't be abstruse.'

He shot out of the sofa, almost spilling the coffee, put it down and went to the bookcase behind her. 'Right,' he said, 'I won't be put down this time.' He pulled out the dictionary after a moment and sat down at the desk with it, just beside her.

'You are looking up the word!' She was touched by this. 'How sweet!'

Sweet!

'So I am hard to understand and profound, am I? That's not me, that's more like you, and whatsisname, Furnace.'

'I didn't quite mean that.'

He looked up from the book. She unexpectedly put an arm on his shoulder, without getting up. He moved towards her, their noses touching.

'And the next word here is for you.'

'What's that?'

'Absurd. You are absurd.'

'Am I? I am very confused.'

Ben set about increasing her confusion.

Normally Andrew wouldn't have knocked, but he felt, for the first time, the need to.

At his knock Ben jumped up and went to open the door. Margot let him, her mind swirling around like cream just added to black coffee.

'Andrew!'

'You!' he said, looking at Ben. 'What are you doing here?'

'Mending the television set,' said Ben, quick as a flash (so he

95

told himself later), 'some wires were crossed,' and went out, downstairs.

Margot found Andrew both abstruse and absurd in the few minutes that followed. Also she found him infuriating. He seemed to be under the impression that Ben had been 'pestering' her and needed admonishing. Although she tried hard to explain to him, she was not quite ready to deliver him the Full Story of her unfortunate liaison with Benny. The story went like this:
> he was stricken with grief, she couldn't help comforting
> him, and the inevitable happened, you know Andrew, how
> softhearted I am, the one thing leading to another and . . .

And she let him rage out of the door after Ben. His protectiveness was *rather* sweet.

Ben was waiting for him on the stairs as a matter of fact, and led him down into the kitchen.
  'Cup of tea, Andrew?' said Benedict, having heard his first name used for the first time, though he had read it often enough.
  'No. Yes. What is all this about?'
  'At the risk of sounding abstruse, all what?'
  'You know what I mean.'
  'Do I?'

Benedict was thinking, and the thought made him smile absurdly, that since Andrew had only ever, to his knowledge, scored six out of ten, while he had scored nine, perhaps he should give him a few tips?

Benedict set the tea things before Andrew and motioned him to sit opposite him at the little table. Andrew sat and reached for the pot, frowning.
  'I don't mind you pouring the tea, being Mum as it were,' said Benedict, 'especially now we know that the blood test was negative. You have to be so careful now. At first it was anyone who had slept with anyone else for four years, then eight, now it's almost a decade. I can't understand why the time gets longer and longer . . .'
  Andrew stared at him.

'But then I am just a simple man. I haven't your education. There are probably all sorts of things you understand which are a mystery to me. For example, it is a mystery to me that one man could find another one attractive, sexually. And some men I am told even like young boys. I have heard tell. Why some of these men are respected pillars of the community: doctors, even lawyers. On the other hand you couldn't fault me on television sets, electrical equipment. Vertical hold gone, I'm your man.'

Andrew stood, more than his vertical hold gone, and turned and walked very deliberately up to the flat. He was shaking.

Benny climbed two at a time when the coast was clear and shot into his bedroom, putting on the earphones, settling back for the matinee performance, his tea in hand.

First there was the creaking of a door and the shuffling of feet on wooden boards. Presumably the audience restless, or the orchestra walking on.
Then Andrew called, shakily, his voice unsteady, for Margot. Enter Margot stage – well it was hard to tell, either side really.

AND: How could you, Margot?
MARG: How could I what?
AND: Don't. Don't do it.
MARG: Do what, for Christ's sake? You look like you've just seen a ghost.
AND: Margot, *what did you tell that man about me?*
MARG: Oh, that. Nothing much, and anyway I changed your name. I changed everyone's names.
AND: Changed my name! What on earth for?
MARG: To protect your identity, you fool . . . Anyway it doesn't matter, he knows about us.
AND: *Knows!* You talk as if there's some intimacy between you. (*A pause.*) Margot!
MARG: Well, I haven't seen you for a while, Andrew, and I haven't had a chance to explain things.
AND: You – and – *him!*
MARG: Well, sort of.
(*Crash! Scrape, shuffle.*)

MARG: Well you had Angela, it's not as if you own me, Andrew. Who are you to throw the first –

AND: Angela is a different thing. Don't compare them. He's not, he's just – a labourer, or – he's not one of *us!*

MARG: Oh I see, it's his class that matters, is it, I should have known. That upset you, does it?

AND: No, I wouldn't mind if it was just some wild impulse to have a bit of rough trade, I could understand it. But you told him about me, and about the AIDS test.

MARG: I did not. I never told anyone about that.

AND: Don't lie to me. He told me.

MARG: That doesn't make any sense. He must have been joking or . . .

AND: Oh, joking, is it?

MARG: What did he actually . . . ?

There was a long pause here, and Benedict moved to the edge of the bed, straining through the earphones, ready to spring. He must not actually let Andrew *harm* her. That was definitely not in the plan.

AND *(quietly)*: You know what this means? This means that you are on your own. Not only is it over between us but all our mutual friends would be horrified. Angela will be horrified. You are cutting yourself off from all that is civilised.

MARG: If your behaviour is what constitutes civilisation, I am glad, then.

AND: I told you to beware that man. I told you he was not to be trusted and you have thrown my advice in my face.

MARG: Well that isn't what I set out to do. In fact I didn't set out to do anything. I just . . . I think I was lonely, Andrew. You were never here.

AND: Just as well I wasn't, it seems.

MARG: If you are going to be like that, you can go away.

AND: I will.

Benedict was waiting by the kitchen, having sprinted down the stairs.

'You haven't had your tea, Andrew.'

98

'So I haven't.' He seemed quite calm now and followed Benny down the hallway. He drank tea. Benny drank tea.

Andrew happened to remark to Benny that some people liked other people to think they were simple and slightly stupid when in fact they were extremely clever, and Benny agreed, adding that there were many ways to skin a cat.

Then Andrew told Benny that he had come to invite Margot to a party, and perhaps he would come also. Benny would be delighted. Andrew wrote down the details.

'I never go to Dorothea's New Year parties.'
'Then now is the time to start.'
'Why?'
'I want to see what *your* friends are like. What *real* friends are.'
'Go on your own, then. I'm not going.'
'I can't do that.'
'Look, Benedict, you have just ruined my entire life, now go away and don't come back!'

Not yet I haven't.

16 *Full Frontal Iseult*

Dorothea liked to think she was famous for her successful parties. Well, we all have our delusions.

Her teenage daughter (a friend of Fiona's as it happens) drew up in her head what must be the definition of her mother's idea of a successful party. She was a girl who had inherited her mother's facility for words and her father's distrust of humanity.

First a Woman must be got in to tidy the house and polish it. She must be a foulmouthed chain-smoker with a bandage of dirty nylon round her head; an enemy to all Children – able to demolish a model or a neatly stacked pile of homework with one destructive swish. Secondly, several boxes of glasses must be hired so that no good ones get broken; thirdly, the drink itself must be ordered and argued about and ordered again. Controversy arose because Dorothea did not make it her business to know about wines – that was the job of her husband who always, wisely, contrived to be in Dar es Salaam each New Year.

Then, on the morning of the party, attempts must be made to ensure that you and your brothers are Out Of The House for the duration. There are several friends you would not normally deign to speak to, one of whom she will arrange for you to spend the night with. No amount of arguing or offering to help will be tolerated.

But there are ways of ensuring you have chicken-pox, mumps, bad stomach cramps, etc. on the day. One of her brothers had actually managed the astonishing feat of breaking his foot one Christmas, but his pleasure at being allowed to sit in the kitchen all evening was dulled by Dorothea Tippexing the obscenities off his 'pot' as they called it – nothing annoyed her like Sheffieldisms – moments before the first guests arrived.

You must all look the part – heaven knows what part she was supposed to play – but in her case it meant that she must look five years younger than she was wont to do. Her mother, too, tried for this effect, though in her case the age-lag was more like twenty years.

Strange to relate, though your teenage daughter looks 'tarty' with a faint and tasteful wash of pink eyeshadow over the rim of her crowfootless eyelid, eighteen times as much make-up, in four different colours (there is no attempt to make a relationship between, say, the eyes and cheeks) applied to your mother's face, together with that awful stapling to attention of the eye-lashes, simply enhances her gracefulness. Her *élan*. The upstairs of the house is thick with the formaldehyde of hairspray (who needs to sniff anything in this house, you can get high by pecking Mother's earlobe) but the downstairs smells of polish and Mozart.

The first guests will arrive early (some people have no *taste*) and will consist of nonentities who are Something in Insurance, or In Banking, or, worse, Writing a Play.

It will be at first lovely, nice, agreeable, charming, enchanting, delightful to see them; then it will be outstanding, superb, magnificent, fantastic, glorious, marvellous, splendid, terrific, super, magic, ace, consummate, and she would have been devastated to greet the New Year without them especially as Jack has as usual failed to get home in time. It seemed the government had more of a hold over his heart than his family. She said this
100

every year. It was never brill or crucial, Iseult noticed. Her mother never used real current words just old worn out ones. Suitable really.

As the crowds of old worn out people (none of them under twenty in the slightest bit) in the honed rooms gathered, thickened, filled the room with smoke, dropped ash and crumbs onto the priceless Berber carpet, Iseult's crippling stomach cramps disappeared and she threaded her way between the clumps with trays of 'nothing really just titbits from the deli down the road'.

Or, translated Iseult, we live in the sort of area where delis abound and I'm too preoccupied with Important Matters ever to enter my own kitchen.

'Do have some radioactive smoked salmon *canopies* – fresh from the Chernobyl-soaked Highland streams.'

'What?'

'Or, more down to earth, the sausage rolls – enriched with steroids and antibiotics from birth. Go on, don't be shy.'

'Come, Margot dear, introduce me to your young man. I didn't catch your name. Someone said you were in television – is that right?'

'Yes.'

'What exactly do you do?'

Margot's heart stopped. What would he say? Everyone in the room stopped talking, put their glasses down, and stepped a foot nearer to hear. We want to know, they chanted, we want to know.

No, they didn't. But Margot found she was suddenly a prey to her worst imaginings. And she had not yet had enough to drink not to care.

Margot was not simply ashamed to have Benedict in tow, but found her nerves were just not up to the event. Her affair with Benedict was a private thing – not that she shared Andrew's sentiments about 'polite society' in the least – it was simply that they were there as a couple and yet she knew so little about him. She was scared, and her fright took the form of skulking about the walls of rooms not really listening to some young man telling her about his latest play nor able to contribute anything to

101

conversations in play about her. Hence began a sort of subjugation to Ben, who seemed more at home here than she had been in his local pub. It was as if his mother's death had unlocked something in him – something always dormant – and he could triumph easily over her.

She did not see Andrew, across the room, guessing as to what was happening, mock-guffawing into his drink, but, crucially as Iseult would say, Benny *did* and so replied, 'Ah, it's very *technical* as a matter of fact.'

The talk resumed, the world sighed and realigned itself.

'Oh, that's beyond me I'm afraid.'

Margot need not have panicked. Dorothea was taking in and retaining less than half of one per cent of anything anyone said to her. Benny might have owned up to being the man who changed the contraceptives in the washrooms in the Swedish Massage Parlour at the other end of town and Dorothea would have confessed to a sad but genteel ignorance of the world of rubber. While giving a professionally convincing imitation of someone concentrating intensely on what you were saying, she was in fact glazed over inwardly, her mind elsewhere.

Only the presence of Iseult nipping about with trays of food roused her temporarily from her preoccupation.

'Iseult for heaven's sake, put that down and go into the kitchen. You are not meant to be here. This is my event and your father will be here any minute and will not want to find you up.'

'I thought he was in Dar es Salaam, Mum.'

'He has only been in Paris, and don't call me that.'

'Sorry, Dorothea.'

Iseult tried to eavesdrop on a conversation to see whether these people made any sense at all. For her pains she was rewarded with one woman trying to explain to another why rich people in Bournemouth did *not* want swimming-pools.

Then she found a Real Person in the kitchen. In her own kitchen! A black woman with beaded dreadlocks and a neat outfit (baggy striped top and tight white leggings) was playing with a small baby. Iseult offered her tea, coffee, biscuits, crisps, a baby-sitting contract for life, and a watch of her own colour television.

'Just get me some of that Spring Water will you while I feed him.'

Iseult cantered off into the dining-room, weighing up the benefits to Baby, via the mammaries, of Scottish radioactivity, Malvern granite-radon gases, or French Château Nuclear Power-station discharge. Malvern it was.

Benedict's body was crying out for a beer. Just a simple beer. He had been offered champagne, vermouth, very potent mulled wine cup, but in reply to a request for beer had been told to 'try the fridge.' Bumbling into the kitchen, he encountered Sally, breastfeeding the baby.

Sharon had breastfed the boys, for ten months each exactly, she had told him proudly. But he had not witnessed it. Many men have never witnessed breastfeeding, either because none has happened in their vicinity due to the proliferation of bottles, or because they have been sent out of the room. Benedict did not realise until this moment what a loss that had been.

Sitting in the middle of a stripped oak pew on a dotted blue cushion, a black woman in startlingly white clothes was curled in a half-moon over a rocking sucking shape at her breast. There seemed to be no particular point where mother ended and child began, only a concentric set of circles with the small bright eyes of the child riveted on hers, in the midst of a moon-bow of sparkling light playing about at the edge of the outer circle, from beads within the dark jute-like strands of her hair, which swayed slightly in time with the inward-outward rocking of the baby.

Had Marian artists so depicted the Mother and Child, the world would be full of Catholics. Well, more full. For Sally is an unthinkable image of Mother Mary: a dateless carbon negative of that powdery blue and corpse-white not-woman. She has large features in tension with each other, a luxuriant fullness of face and brightness of eye and her smooth elastic skin is very, very black.

*

103

'I only wanted a beer,' Benny said, hardly able to speak, so stirred did he feel, so full of amazement. Of reverence. He wanted to kneel down and intone something to them.

'It's OK, I don't mind,' she said, looking up for a moment and down again. Rapt, adoring.

Did my mother, thought Benny, did Bet? And found a can of lager, ice-cold in the fridge.

A girl, the daughter with the silly name, ran in with a glass of water.

Benny sat down on the pew, too close for politeness. He felt inexplicably at ease.

'Do you mind?' he asked.

'No. Do you want to watch? People aren't used to it nowadays.'

'I think Dorothea put us all straight onto puréed steak and smoked salmon at birth,' said Iseult, sitting herself down on the other side of Sally.

'Well, this is nice,' said Sally, laughing, 'and I wasn't even invited.'

'Neither was I really,' said Ben.

'I should have guessed,' said Iseult, 'gatecrashers! All my life I've been waiting for someone to gatecrash Dorothea's party. And now two at once. It's staggering.'

Since Iseult declared shortly that she was going to have twenty-five children and live on a farm with goats, Sally allowed her to change the baby's nappy. This she did with great gusto and made Sally and Ben laugh.

Sally did not want Iseult to think she really was a gatecrasher so she explained that she had come along as gooseberry to a couple, one of whom she shared a flat with. She also explained that from tomorrow onwards she was to have the flat to herself at last because her flatmate was moving in with the boyfriend. And how she needed the space! So, to celebrate, and so that she and Enoch would not be on their own at the turning of the year, she had come with them to the party.

She was surprised at how Benny laughed at this.

'What's so funny?'

'I've just realised who you are. And Enoch?' he said. 'How could you?'

'Oh that, just a joke.'

'I think people should have ordinary names,' said Iseult de CranBerry Vivaise.

'Well he'll be Eno to his friends.'

Benny was wondering whether he had been instrumental in Sally's altered expectations or not. If not, then Andrew was a better faker and bigger scoundrel than he had thought.

Iseult suddenly had what she thought was a grown-up notion. It was that she should leave these two relatively old people together because Eno had no father and they seemed to like each other's company.

'Would you excuse me, I must go and help my poor old mum with the drinks etc. My father never turns up until the eleventh hour.'

Iseult's self-sacrifice was rewarded with the most dreadful put-down from her mother who made some remark about Sindy dolls which cut her to the quick.

It was foolish of Dorothea to do so, for her daughter was her match verbally and said, 'Mummy *does* know how old I am, contrary to appearances, and was not a child bride. Hence when she says 34 she is probably confused and means 34B, mistaking size for age. In fact her age has been upwardly mobile from her bra size for some time now.'

Ah, the price of a liberal education!

Dorothea found herself explaining to three couples too young to care that the important thing with teenagers was to make them think independently, even at your own expense sometimes. They thought that independence must mean getting away with embarrassing/insulting your parents and two women there silently vowed never to reproduce.

Benny found four more lagers, persuaded Iseult to take Baby Enoch upstairs to watch television, and danced an improvised

105

tango with Sally in the Dancing Area between the dining-room and the lounge.

Margot saw them and wondered at his self-confidence. She didn't like it but was dancing with J. at the time. Andrew and Angela had snuck off somewhere and it was some time before she was able to get Benedict on his own and ask if he was ready to go home.

He was not. He thought she was right: her friends were much nicer than his, in fact he hadn't had so much fun for ages. At one point, infuriated, she even found him sharing a joke with Andrew, newly arrived from the downstairs games room where some people had retired to play snooker.

Seeing her get her fiftieth drink from the dining-room, Andrew bent over her (rather sinister now) and said into her ear, 'Ben's not so bad, I take it all back,' then he spilt a plate full of coleslaw and hummus onto the floor.

'Oh shit. Could you clear it up for me? Angie's waiting for me downstairs.'

'I've found someone who can waltz!' shouted Dorothea to the world in general.

Being able to dance many dances perfectly, thanks to the Over-60s Tea Dances, Ben was armed as no one else could be to sweep the hostess literally off her feet. Looking after Bet had been one long rehearsal and now he could shed a skin like a snake and come out in full colour at last. He was surprised too to find, after the fifth drink, that Margot's friends (which they mostly were not) were no better nor worse than his own: they simply had more wealth to enjoy – and why not?

Dorothea and Benedict glided across the hallway and into the dining-room, where there was more space. Benny could foxtrot, paso doble, jive, and quickstep too. But Dorothea had only learnt to waltz, in case someone of note ever asked her to in public. It was also an impressive display she had been known to mount with her (still absent) husband for the benefit of sixth formers at the Annual Ball.

'Trust me,' said Ben, 'just fall back, I'll catch you.' So they
106

became more and more exaggerated, less and less like the Over-60s in any way. Dorothea was panting loudly and gasping for a fag by the time, ten minutes to midnight, her husband walked in, a suitcase in either hand.

Iseult arrived with Enoch in her arms and did not understand her father's joke about not knowing she even had a black boyfriend and the Pill.

Sally took him over in the midst of the howls of drunken laughter, and they gathered round the television for the countdown.

On the periphery of the group Ben asked Sally what she wished for the New Year and she said, 'A secure roof over my head and no more housing problems,' and he kissed her on the lips and wished her that. Andrew made sure to kiss both Angela and Margot, who was departing towards Benedict despite herself. She had seen, and made an unfortunate remark about, how he seemed to find motherhood a turn-on, to which he replied that he hated a pissed woman, to which she replied that she thought he rather liked it, judging by the night before she went away. But the smile he gave her and the implied intimacy of her own remark backfired and she felt belittled somehow. Finally as the tones of Big Ben struck, she found she was wanting Small Ben to make some gesture and took his hand, which he did not withdraw.

You'd think there was no such thing as a Safe Limit or Drink-Driving laws, to see Dorothea's guests taking to their cars in staggering droves of intoxication. You'd think no one had ever died as a result of confusion behind the wheel. You'd think no one knew that you only *think* you drive better tanked up.

Credit to Andrew that he warned people as they did so of the heavy fines, possible prison sentences and forbade Margot to drive home. It was a two-mile walk from Dorothea's home, but he insisted, threatening to throw her keys down the nearest drain. After all, he said, he was her legal representative. Benny found this most amusing.

*

So they set off as a group: Andrew and Angela, Benedict and Margot, and Sally with Baby Enoch, in a pouch on her back, fast asleep at last. Sally could not stop herself from informing Margot that wearing fur was a moral issue but Margot replied that the coat had belonged to her grandmother, and so the animals had died ever so long ago. They sang all the way, songs like 'We all Live in a Yellow Submarine' and 'Whenever you Need a Friend, I'll be There', and 'Bridge Over Troubled Water' resounded around the quiet and tree-lined avenue of Dore, and then the hilly Victorian slopes of semi-posh Broomhill and then finally, under the lime trees of Psalter Lane itself. Here Benny finally disentangled himself from Sally around whom his arms had been draped, and from Angela who had been snuggling under his arm on his other side and he and Margot split off from them as they went the last few hundred yards towards the park, and Angela's flat, where they were all three to spend the very last night.

In the hall, Benny turned to double lock the door and they faced each other. An ordinary couple 'living together' might now have wandered into their bedroom, fallen on the bed and fallen asleep: or they could drink a mug of coffee each, post-morteming the party before going to bed. But Benny and Margot are not an ordinary couple living together. They live in the same house, they sleep together sometimes, but they share no kitchens, and increasingly, Margot fears, no common ground. They did not so much live together as adjacent.

Margot starts up the stairs, slowly Benny follows. At his floor he stops and walks towards his room.

'Ben?'

'Yes, what?'

'Nothing.'

17 *Diary 2*

Thursday 1st January, 1987.
Woke up alone this a.m. The year clear and frosty over Northern England. Somewhere in the world people are warm and happy. On the flip side of the planet, in Australia for instance.

Dorothea's party the disaster I anticipated, only worse. B.

108

behaved abom: snuck off with black friend Angela's, found them, her boobs hanging out, tête-à-tête in kitchen, later dancing. Also sweeping Dorothea about the floor in a sort of waltz. Determined to embarrass me? He and Andrew seem pals now. Men can't help conspiring against women.

But worst news is that Angela is moving in with Andrew. This really kills me. He must be doing it to spite me because he said many times that he would *never* live with anyone except me. Now he seems to have suggested it to Angie (so she says) in order to give Sally more room! So casual a move. How could he? And Angela is as thick as two planks. It won't last. It will, that's the trouble.

There's nothing men like more than Dumb Dames. Who am I kidding? I have been too demanding of everyone.

And Ben – what is he up to? – he might be *using* me as a means to social advancement. Why does he know how to behave in my world when I'm such a disaster in his? Perhaps he gets it from the telly.

This is paranoia though. Surely. It's all too easy to imagine they are all in the conspiracy against me. Sally, Angie, Andrew, Dorothea, everyone. But of course they aren't and there's probably something wrong with me. PMT?

What shall I resolve for the solstice? Give Benny the Boot? Find somewhere else to live? Murder Dorothea? Murder Andrew? Angela? Sally? Oh God, what a way to start the New Year.

I resolve to think positively about everything and everyone, starting now.

I am not pregnant. I have not got AIDS. I have not got Christianity. I am not unemployed. I am not homeless. What a lucky person I am! (Good try.)

Friday 2nd January
Tried to spend yesterday planning lessons and failed. But by afternoon my curiosity overcame me and I went down to see what Ben was doing. He was reading with the headphones on, on his bed.

In my new positive mood I asked him if he wanted anything, meaning lunch, cup of tea etc., and he said, yes, there were lots of things he wanted. Like what? Couldn't I guess? No.

109

A baby. He wants a baby!

At first I just laughed but he stared out of the window so forlornly I had to believe he meant it. Felt like running away, such crazy idea. But more we spoke about it, more I see he has it worked out. His plan is that I should take statutory maternity leave and then he will look after it from then on, full time, repairing the occasional TV in the evenings if we need the money. We could do up the house and move down into it, and even rent out the upstairs flat – we wouldn't need it.

All so neat. And then he hit the sore nerve in me, saying he thought I would soon start to regret being over thirty if I didn't have a child, and not many men would take it on, the way he was offering. We would marry if I wanted to, it made no difference to him.

I told him I was against marriage, and found I was talking about the subject as if it were feasible.

Four hours later, writing this, I still feel excruciatingly excited by the idea, as if some searing seed has been planted in the centre of my brain and is sending out shoots to all corners. Everything else I try to think of is influenced by this thought: a baby.

A baby would anchor me in the real world and give my whole life meaning.

Or it could be the most stupid idea which ever entered my brain.

Saturday 3rd January
Such a laugh last night. Ben was sitting on my sofa when I came back from shopping, wearing only my fur coat! He insisted on unpacking the food to show how domestic he can be and then we tossed the diaphragm (dome we do, hollow we don't) and I laughed so much at this that I could hardly take his passion seriously. However, have almost come to my senses *re* having a baby and realise it is just a whim. You can't have a baby for the reason that you might regret not having one. That is, as Angela would say, putting the cart before the horse.

All this emotional turmoil is delaying my period (ironically).

Tuesday 6th January
(5 days late)

Back to school. Dorothea announced that her husband has landed a post so prestigious she cannot tell us what it is or where it is, but that she has decided to join him and set up home there. Wherever it is. She will stay until end of Summer Term, and then leave. GERONIMO! I won't have to murder her.

Angela cancelled our jogging – not like her. Relieved, though.

Hope you are not angry with me, she says. Oh no, I said, on the contrary: so glad you have taken Andrew on permanently.

Saturday 10th January
Angela phoned this morning, she wanted me to be the first to know. She has had a positive pregnancy result. Andrew is thrilled.

They will marry in three weeks time. Apparently Andrew was just waiting for an excuse to Really Settle Down. Why didn't I think of this? Guess I am not ruthless enough. Tried to sound happy for them, but felt only resentment, jealousy even.

This really couldn't have been better for Ben than if he had engineered it himself. What am I saying? All my resolve *re* being sensible out the bloody window.

I AM THIRTY AND ONE HALF AND CHILDLESS. SHIT.

18 *The Power of Prayer*

Margot's mother had informed God that her daughter needed to have a baby. This is the sort of request He likes. It is one of His better party pieces – making virgins swell with child, the elderly who had just agreed to surrogate motherhood conceive themselves, those who had given up and adopted, and so on.

Obviously God is no psychoanalyst, whatever Freud would have us believe, for he seldom delves into motives. Neither will I about Mary or Sarah, or . . . but Margot's mother's motives are of interest to us. She thinks that she is wishing upon her daughter something crucial for her spiritual well-being: an interest outside herself, a possibility of renewal, before it is too late. I think she is grieving for the family who have left her – her husband for another world (we shan't debate it here) and Margot because of her conversion. And like Benedict, she is unable to express her grief and so transmutes it, into a desire to be a grandmother.

There is of course nothing ignoble in this desire, and it is perhaps the most universally acceptable desire. What is unacceptable is that so *netted* is Margot's mother by the Pioneer Chapel that she cannot simply say to God please give me a grandchild soon. She has to ask for something for Margot. Of course there is no question of her simply ringing Margot up and saying why don't you stop taking the Pill and get on with it. She has been under the impression, wrongly, that Margot has been on the Pill for ten years.

Suffice it to say that either God answered Margot's mother's prayers, or Mother Nature fiddled with her menstrual cycle at the time of Benny's attack (I go for this theory myself), or the black holes came to the aid of the Unborn, waiting, as Africans think, to be born, or for no reason whatsoever a particular sperm at a particular time made the acquaintance of a particular egg and set in motion that random sequence of inevitability called Early Morning Sickness.

For one morning (16th January) Benedict realised that Margot had not gone to work yet, although it was nine o'clock. He found her vomiting in the bathroom. She asked him to phone Dorothea and say she would be late.

Of course he looked after her. Brought her breakfast from her kitchen. Puffed up her pillows so like he used to for Bet.

She says her breasts feel tender. Shall he call the doctor? No, she knows what it is and it's all his fault. Don't worry, I'll take care of you. It's what I'm best at.

The snow fell and fell and Ben made delicious little breakfasts for her before she went to work, wrapped her warmly and drove her to and from work. He even attached slip-proof runners to her winter boots so that she would not slip on the ice along the ginnels by the school, and cleared the path and salted it, as he had done for Bet previous years. Two days a week he made her eat liver and spinach; he read about and put into practice modern theories on roughage and vitamins and minerals, and carefully filtered bottles of water for her to drink, while drinking from the tap himself.

112

19 *Enemy Number One*

'Let's opt for a Caesarean,' said Ben.

They were sitting at the back of a dingy hall, having watched the film about birth for prospective parents. Frankly, so unremittingly gory had the film been that Margot had wished she could change her mind that very moment. The moment when the blood-streaked football had split the surrounding flesh to enter the screen, to the cries of terminal anguish from the woman at the other end of the trauma.

Then there had been a quick Alternative Procedure whereby a surgeon made a small incision and lifted a perfect child from its sleeping mother in complete quiet and aseptic splendour. There seemed to be less blood and no anguish whatsoever.

'Seems much more sensible,' said Ben.

'You can't opt. You have no choice. That's for when things go wrong.'

'Seems all backwards to me,' he said.

Ben was Enemy Number One to the midwives. He would always say the obvious rather than the sentimental, unlike most of the other fathers. They knew too that he was going to be the Prime Caretaker (a phrase which ruefully reminded him of landlord) of the child, and had to take him seriously. When he said to Eileen one day as they were leaving that he thought Heavy Metal at full throttle on a ghetto-blaster to drown the cries of the mother would be more appropriate than soft music in the background, she could have killed him. Some of the other would-be fathers found him a welcome relief from the seriousness of everything.

It isn't such a far cry from the incontinence jokes he had once thought up – Ben found himself somehow on familiar territory.

On the other hand Ben seemed to have a natural way with the slippery plastic dolls they practised bathing: This isn't realistic, he'd said, surely the baby will slither about, and have no head control. Couldn't we practise on a real one? You'll have to find one yourself, said Eileen, but you're right, actually.

113

And the bottle-feeding. But I want to breastfeed. Yes, but you never know. In the night, or if you aren't up to it. You'll be getting up in the night will you, Ben? Yes, four-hourly, or three-hourly, or continuously? It won't bother me. I'm used to it.

How do you mean?

Mother.

You had to see to her in the night?

Of course. I only need three hours, minimum, I've worked out.

Perhaps the bottle would be best, then.

On the way home Ben stopped the car outside a shop where he had seen a peculiarly interesting Easter egg. He presented it to Margot. When you tapped the top it broke open in a perfect chocolate incision to reveal another egg which broke open to reveal a small marzipan chick.

The baby was due in late September, so they had the whole spring and summer to prepare. Ben's first move was to remove the Kiddy Alert from Margot's floor and put it back together again. Easter being over and with Margot back at work and in the healthy phase of the pregnancy, not needing so much care and attention, Ben turned to the house. Just as the first foolhardy daffodils were stabbing upwards in the south-facing front patch of Mrs Harrison's front area, he started to gut the lower floor of the house with a view to installing, with the help of a drinking friend, central heating.

The only room he did not modernise in those long spring weeks was Bet's old room. This room he left entirely alone. Otherwise the house began to take on some of its old splendour – some of its old middle-class pretensions. Nothing had been ripped out, though nothing had been done to preserve it either. Tiles around fireplaces were intact though covered with mould. Margot cleaned them up and had the fireplaces opened up, bought firedogs and brass knick-knacks on Saturday mornings in Chesterfield market to stand on the Morris tiled frontages. She made Ben paint everything in shades of white rather than white, and installed more and more plants everywhere.

Margot nailed a piece of rubber draught-proofing against the bottom inside of the front door. Then, picking Geoffrey up by one ear with thumb and forefinger, as if he were contaminated, she marched with him towards the dustbin. Ben stopped her.

'What are you doing with Geoffrey?' he asked.

'Geoffrey!' Margot laughed. Ben did not move other than to take him by the string round his middle. 'We don't need this filthy piece of velvet any more; I have put some modern draught-excluder on the door, like most people have.'

'I don't care what *most* people do, Geoffrey has always been there.'

'I can tell by the *smell*.'

He was on the verge of anger; Margot wondered in a detached sort of way what form his anger would take. It was the first real dispute, of that special domestic and trivial nature which would take some couples three days of sulking to exorcise. Ben saw that she was challenging him to react irrationally and so took the dachshund to the bin outside the back door and as he dropped him in said, 'Goodbye, Geoffrey.'

Margot felt somehow humbled by this, somehow belittled.

'And for my next turn,' said Ben coming back into the kitchen, 'I shall dispose of Mrs Harrison in a similar way.'

Thus he had not only succumbed to her Better Wisdom, but made her laugh into the bargain.

Then finally, one day when she was at work, Ben moved all her furniture, including the bed, and some kitchen cabinets (they were not really fitted) downstairs and when she came home, they had moved into the house proper.

'What will your old room be?'

'The nursery.'

After dinner (Ben had learnt to cook two vegetarian dishes, both with pasta), Ben took out a sheaf of papers from a plastic bag by the front door.

'Andrew has drawn up something for us,' he said.

'Andrew?'

'Andrew Furness.'

'Yes, I know who you mean. I just wondered when . . .'

They sat on the pink sofa, now dwarfed by the size of the front room, acres of grey carpet and the six-foot high fireplace.

'I want you to feel secure,' said Ben.

'That's sweet. You mean now I have lost my sitting tenancy,' she giggled.

He looked at her sternly. 'You have not lost your sitting tenancy at all by moving downstairs.'

'Oh, I thought I had.'

Her own sitting tenant kicked and rocketed about inside her.

'Quick, feel,' she said. He felt nothing, as usual. This infuriated her. Perhaps she only imagined movements?

'If you sign this,' began Ben, 'you will become a joint owner of the house with me.'

'You are giving me?' What . . . what was he giving her, exactly?

'Half the house. That's right.'

'Why? What's the point, Ben?'

'I thought, since we aren't married, it would make you feel more secure, if anything happened to me, that's all. I know it's important to you.' He found the right formula of words by dint of having read her diary of course.

She signed. Then they laughingly divided the house into His and Hers. Since she needed to pee at least every twenty minutes, she thought she had better have the toilet, and he had better have both televisions in case they went wrong.

Ben tied up the sheets and put them back in the envelope, in a drawer of his table in his old room.

20 *Two Ladies*

Everything is in the mind, except what is in the womb, thinks Margot. Now that the world has come right side up, shining, even Dorothea is a Friend. She is just an eccentric middle-aged woman who runs the department, and does it quite well sometimes. She also has very reassuring things to say about pregnancy, childbirth, breastfeeding by remote control, men transmuted into Fatherhood, and so on.

'You couldn't have chosen a better father,' says Dorothea. 'I am sure he will come up trumps as full-time parent – such an energetic young man. You must come to dinner some time.'

*

And Angela is a Fellow Conspirator now.

'Two pregnancies on the staff at once; it must be an epidemic,' said the bald geography master.

'Sperm seldom travels through the air like germs, though I can't vouch for yours,' said Dorothea.

Summer sun, weak and Northern, but bright, filtered down strangely in the sports hall, making bars and shapes shimmer on the parquet floor as if it were once a swimming-pool. Margot spends much of her lunch-hour here with Angela, swapping swollen ankle stories, sleepless nights stories. Somehow the most boring detail of Angela's pregnancy has some vital meaning in relation to her own, though she cannot fathom it.

'No horse-riding, no trampolining, no diving – I'm a bit stymied,' said Angela one day. 'It's getting increasingly difficult to do my job. Still it won't be for much longer.'

'Aren't you going to carry on then?'

'No, Andrew won't want me to go back to work afterwards. There's no point anyway . . . Who would look after the baby?'

'Ah, yes. A childminder? No, I see your point. Won't you get very bored?'

Margot had assumed for some reason that she and Angela would go on swapping notes and being In It Together after the birth, but of course Angela was not coming back.

'No, it's what I always aimed for. Lady of leisure – with sprogs.'

'Angela – was it, you know, deliberate?'

'No, not exactly, but I did think there was no point being on the Pill for years and years if you were going to have to use condoms for protection against AIDS anyway.'

'So you . . . ?'

'Well . . . sort of. Didn't you?'

'No!'

'Well, pardon me for living.' She often said dumb things like 'pardon me for living', 'excuse my French', etc. How could Andrew put up with it?

'Oh, come on, Marg, let's do these exercises. Got to be primed for action. Don't want to be caught napping.'

They got on all fours, in the staff sports room, and arched and rounded their backs, like a couple of first years pretending to be

117

horses in Drama. They always ended up rolling about on the mats laughing.

Angela stared up at the polystyrene squares above her and said, 'I've given up booze and fags and jogging and Casual Sex and I think for that I deserve to Be Forgiven for everything and I also deserve an easy birth.'

Superstitiously, Margot hoped she would have a hard one, so that she herself would have an easy one. As if there were a finite number of easy births available in the universe, and Angela must not use them up.

'Oh, I hope you do. Andrew going to be there?'

"I wouldn't miss it for the world, dear," he says. Bringing the video camera too! You'll be the first to see the film, promise.'

'Can't wait.'

A bell rang and like trained dogs, they put on their stern faces and went to face Afternoon Registration.

Margot had the fifth form and found that she had gone up in their estimation enormously now that she was Expecting an Illegitimate Child. And not even married! Tremendous!

For once she was brill, crucial, and fab (hadn't she heard that one somewhere before?) and didn't even have to do anything to gain all the admiration.

Large spotty youths she had earmarked as 'violent tendencies' in secret school reports now carried her piles of books around and shy girls asked her after morning prayers if the baby had moved yet and what names she had thought of.

Why does your pregnancy soften the whole world? And why was it the answer to world wars? Should all world leaders be pregnant women about to give birth – would the world be a better place? So Margot's mind drifted all afternoon watching over the Lower Sixth revising in a cold sweat in the bright July heat.

Today the US President and her Russian equivalent sat down round the conference table to discuss disarmament, cultural relations and episiotomies. Braxton Hicks featured largely on

118

the agenda also. Several doctors and midwives were in attendance and advised the two about the relative merits of breastfeeding and bottle-feeding. Both agreed that nuclear
disarmament would be Best for Baby and details will be drawn
up in the post-natal week. News reporters were waiting in the
wings for any news and – ah – the world leaders have agreed
to name their babies Medium-range and Multilateral, with
patronymics made up of each other's names.
Two United Nations military bands played lullabies in salute as
the two women left to attend their respective labour wards . . .

'Miss could we have the window open, I think I'm going to faint.'

Ben always met her from work now, with the car. He was in the
process of selling it. They decided together (and how nice now,
not to have to make Unilateral Decisions any more) that she had
outgrown a sports car and they needed a Family Saloon so that
the carry-cot could be safely harnessed onto the back seat.
    Today he seemed to be in a dream, as so often. Margot had
thought being pregnant (what he wanted after all) would bring
them closer together and was quite surprised, though even
Dorothea has reassured her that men are moody, worry about
the birth, etc., that he seemed more distant. Perhaps it was
because they so seldom made love. At first it was dangerous, she
had agreed with that. Then he did not want to 'tax' her, though
she was willing enough. Gradually they drifted into a routine of
not making love at all, simply falling asleep after the last movie
of the evening, together, in her hard bed, on the front side of the
first storey of the house. Ben would horse around with her as if
they were brother and sister – joking about Reasons Not To:
there were no mirrors to inspire him, he was of an age when he
had to conserve his strength (you do know I'm nearly eighty,
he'd say), or there is no room in the bed for you, me and the
Bulge.
    But the increasingly hot nights made her restless and weary,
and she found herself reading six-hundred-page trashy books,
lent to her by Angela, way into the night.

Of course time is different now; nothing is so urgent. You cannot
live one day at a time when you are launched on a forty-week

119

block of time which will deliver you into a new life at the end of it, which is the beginning of everything, whether you will or not. There is no changing your mind, no resigning. Ben wanted this child, more than she did, so she often thought, so there was no question of his giving up, moving on, disappearing. So, in a way, nothing mattered any more, not urgently.

While Margot was at work, Ben kept those floors of the house in use pristine clean (as if a birth were to happen there) and read, picking up speed, all Margot's books, even the ones she had not read herself. He began to want to discuss with someone his thoughts about all these books, but in the evenings they ate dinner, Margot marked, and then it was time for bed. Even at the weekends when there would have been time, she didn't *want* to discuss the literature she had been teaching all week. She simply wanted to eat, read baby books, sleep and watch television. While she did so Ben read the *Guardian* cover to cover, barring only the job advertisements.

At first Margot had attempted to read her *Times Lit. Supp.* and her *Literary Review*, but found it hard to concentrate on anything but *Breast is Best* and *Babylove*. She also read and reread pamphlets given her at the ante-natal clinic on the stages of labour and allied subjects. But her periodicals were read from cover to cover – by Ben. Margot could only remember ever having seen one baby – a black one – and could not imagine motherhood: hence she read up on it endlessly.

'I don't see why you bother to read the paper,' said Margot one day, 'the nine o'clock news will tell you what's been going on in the world, if that concerns you, though I can't think why it should.'

Ben brightened – this was tantalisingly close to the opportunity he had been longing for to expound one of his latest theories.

'No, it's different news, according to the media. You see the television will give you the news which it has some film of, something visual, whether or not it's really important. The radio gives more foreign news but only from those places where they have a correspondent. But the newspaper is supreme – you get all that and people who specialise in the subject telling you *why* what has happened, has. Do you see what I mean? It's not *what* but *why* that matters.'

120

'Hmmm.' Margot had drifted off to sleep. She dreamt that Ben had left her and was going to some foreign part to become a foreign correspondent for the *Guardian*, and woke suddenly in a sweat.

'What were you saying, Ben?'

'Never mind.'

Mrs Harrison was having a field day, weeks of field days. She was more than happy to publicise first the details of the renovations which Young Benedict had carried out, now that his Poor Old Mother could no longer benefit from them, and equally, if not more, pleased to inform the neighbourhood that the purpose of all this expense was to give everyone the impression that he and the Lodger, who was at least five months 'gone', were a proper married couple.

Mrs Patel, on the other hand, stood one day at her door, having swept the step, when Benny was returning with groceries, and stared at him.

'Hello there, Mrs Patel. Better weather we're having now, isn't it?'

'You married that girl, Mr Ashe?'

'No. She didn't want to get married.'

'It isn't right.' She almost spat at him, turning, with the broom behind her like a blunt staff, back into the house.

Benny felt unaccountably depressed all day. Why should it matter what she thought?

21 *Medals*

The school assembly hall had been designed, albeit recently, on feudal lines. The Headmaster had a semicircle of his own above the rest of the staff too senior to have forms. The plebs sat in rows on the floor three feet down, each four rows with a seated junior teacher at the end. Behind them were the sixth form, on chairs. The acoustics in the hall were so bad that Margot had refused ever to put on a performance there. Everyone's voice boomed, their sibilants exploded, their hesitations seemed monumental.

This late July day, the end of term, they had just watched the

sixth form play – a cruel caricaturing of the teachers' eccentricities, to howls of laughter from the lower ranks, and even some
of the teachers. Margot had not noticed herself in the production
and wondered whether that was because she was not particularly
popular or because she could not recognise her own eccentricities
when magnified like this.

Now what she was dreading. The presentations to teachers
who were retiring or leaving for 'greater things' at other schools,
or to have babies. These presentations seemed to be in order of
seniority, and Margot was distressed that Angela went up the
four feet before her. However the Head was notably diplomatic
and announced her as a teacher 'who was leaving the school
only temporarily on maternity leave'. A member of her own
form, a girl, came forward with a small present and gave it to
her. There was clapping as there had been for Angela, but it was
muted. She wondered whether this indicated that she was less
popular (hadn't Angela done marvellous things with the netball
team after all, and introduced trampolining) or whether they all
secretly thought it wrong of her to continue working after she
had produced the baby?

22 *Peace Treaties*

At nine o'clock on Sunday morning the ninth of August, Andrew
phoned Ben and Margot to say he was the proud father of a baby
boy born three hours earlier and weighing six pounds, three and
half ounces, and the half-ounce was all hair! Bright red like his
own. He had filmed the crucial bits and Angela was fine, dying
for visitors this afternoon.

Margot found it difficult to hide her depression. Not only had it
been a straightforward birth, it was a boy! Now she would have
a hard time and a girl. Suddenly she realised how badly she
wanted a boy.

'But I long for a girl,' said Ben, uncharacteristically animated
this morning. 'I don't want a boy at all.'

'You don't want a son?' she asked him.

'No. Not at all.'

122

'But I thought all men wanted a son.'

'I'm not all men, as I keep telling you.'

Later, helping her out of the car, a four-door saloon, one year old, in which Ben had already drilled holes for the safety harnesses, Ben had a flash of insight, looking at her face, downcast and bitter.

'You don't still hanker after Andrew, do you?'

'What?'

'You don't wish, that you . . . ?'

She laughed, tears in her eyes, 'How could you say that? Ben, I love you, you know that.' She started to weep. This was nothing new. Often she wept uncontrollably for no apparent reason. Ben locked the car and put his arm around her.

'It's just the hormones. Makes you vulnerable,' and he led her across the car-park to the front doors of the hospital, thinking that a few months ago he would never have dared to use a word he had only read, like 'vulnerable' . . .

It was not what she wanted him to say. He never had said it, and she feared that he might not ever say it.

'I'm in love,' said Angela the moment they spotted her, one of four women sitting up, obviously waiting for visitors. Andrew was not there.

'Angela, congratulations,' said Margot, with a croaky voice. 'How was it?'

'Brilliant. Only six hours in labour, and no stitches. And he's adorable. Andrew better watch out, I'm head over heels for him. Here he comes. Get a load of this!' Ben handed her the freesias.

Andrew approached wheeling what looked like a transparent plastic sculpture of a shopping trolley in front of him. Inside was a pile of sheets, the object of their pride.

Angela pronounced herself to be too jealous of her son to let anyone but Margot have a small hold (just for practice) and then unwrapped him, exposing his slightly greasy whiteness and red hair, offered a distended breast and attached him to it. He suckled noisily, and she winced.

'Does it hurt then?' asked Margot, genuinely surprised.

123

'Not really, it's just that I get a slight tummy ache when he starts sucking.'

'That's afterpains; the uterus is contracting,' said Ben. They all stared at him.

'Ben's been reading up on things,' said Margot, by way of apology.

'Well if we need any advice then,' said Andrew, 'we'll know where to come.'

Then they told between them the Story of the Birth in more detail than Margot, or anyone, would ever want to have. Down to the very words the midwife said when she started to push, no that was when I was still panting, no we were doing the candle breathing then. No.

Ben was amused. He wondered, what with helping breathe and push and relax, how Andrew had had the time to take the film.

Then Sally arrived, minus Baby Enoch, whom she had left with a neighbour. She exclaimed over the infant in suitably exaggerated terms, which was what both parents had been wanting. She declared him to be the most beautiful (white) baby ever born, the most intelligent looking, the wisest, and so on. Margot thought it ridiculous, but Angela and Andrew simply thought it was the obvious response to their offspring.

Then, putting him back to the breast, to which he already seemed well addicted, Sally advised Angela not to poke her breast with a finger to stop him suffocating – it would only give her a blocked duct and he wouldn't suffocate.

It was only when Ben and Margot were leaving, and offered Sally a lift, that she confided her trouble in them. The landlord was trying to evict her. Apparently he did not mind her being the sub-tenant of Angela but he objected for some reason to her being the sole tenant.

'Is it because you're black or because you're unmarried?' asked Ben.

Margot was embarrassed and said, 'Ben!'

'He claims I haven't paid enough rent, and sends back my cheques.'

They took her home.

124

'Why don't we offer Sally our flat?' asked Ben, when they were home.

'*My* flat you mean.'

'All right, why don't we offer her your flat? We don't need it. It's just empty space. She could live here with Enoch.'

There was no failure of imagination in Margot's consideration of this proposal. She could imagine all too well the company that it would provide for Ben when she was out at work and he was at home, like Sally, with a baby. It would be so easy for them. The vision of Sally's beautiful ebony breast dangling a few inches from him in Dorothea's kitchen had made quite an impression on her.

'But we don't want a sitting tenant, do we? We might need the space one day.'

'What for?'

'Well, suppose I didn't go back to work and we had to take in lodgers or something. You might want a workshop one day, or we might have six more children.'

These fantastic suggestions were indication to Ben that she was hunting for reasons, when in fact she had simply decided to veto the idea.

'I can see the idea does not appeal to you, so I'll drop it.'

Of course there were no fireworks. There were never words shouted in anger, never any opportunity for real eloquence (she could grind him into the dust surely with her eloquence).

Not that Margot could actually admit to herself that she missed that soul-wrenching experience: rows; but she did miss the *reconciliation*. With Andrew, and previous men, she had taken this rowing as an indication of how deeply they cared about her, about what she thought and said. With Ben it must mean that he simply *knew* she was more likely to be right than he; because of her background, her education. It could not mean that he did not care. That was not possible. You don't set up a life and produce a child with someone you don't care for. Do you? Only once had she seen the fireworks he was capable of, that night at the pub when she had drunk too much and suddenly felt she was with someone else. It was possibly, she had calculated, that very night on which she had conceived. But she didn't like to think that: conceived in anger.

*

Over the next few weeks, into the start of the new term, while she waited, Margot visited Angela often. She saw her turn into a most proficient mother. Jasper slept Like an Angel, fed Like a Trooper, seldom cried and delighted everyone, especially his four grandparents who came at regular intervals to coo over him, and invest precious gifts, hand-knitted items and so on.

Andrew was 'marvellous' with Jasper, though he only needed to be marvellous for about half an hour a day since he came home from work half an hour before he went down for the night.

Of course Angela did not expect him to deal with nappies or any of the difficult things, and there was no *need* for him to get up at night since she had the breasts and he needed to be at work at nine a.m. It would be nice though, she admitted on about Margot's fourth visit when they had finally got round to watching the video of the birth, if he would wash up occasionally. But by the fifth visit, they had a dishwasher awkwardly jammed in between the washing-machine and the fridge. So again, there was no *need*. Who stacks it, then, asked Margot. Oh I do. Well I'm here more than he is, aren't I?

How they had rowed about that, Angela giggled! If you had servants to do everything for you, you'd argue about who was to give them the orders!

'So the device doesn't really solve the underlying problem?' asked Margot.

'What underlying problem?'

'The thing which makes you argue all the time.'

'It's not *all* the time. There's no underlying problem. Everyone rows now and then, don't they?'

Margot drew out her silky little trump card and laid it on the table with her manicured fingertips. 'Benny and I never row.'

'Never?'

Angela went into school to show Jasper off, as if he were an award or certificate you show at assembly.

After her visit she was able to tell Margot that Dorothea was still there because although her husband had gone to wherever it was, she was staying to sell the house, which was proving difficult. They had taken on a new member of the English department as a temporary measure, but J. had been asked to do the Drama!

Sometimes Margot would tell Ben of her visits to Angela as a way of expressing her fears as to what might go wrong. He was always at pains to point out three things to her: one, that she was not like Angela; two, that he was not like Other Men; and three, that she would not have to stay at home all day loading the dishwasher and listening to Radio Four, since he would be doing that. Then he would smile and nuzzle her bump with which he was already on most affectionate terms, and say, 'And I shall do it all *gladly.*'

How could there be anything aggressive, anything sinister about that *gladly*? How could she rid herself of that primitive, unliberated possessiveness which seemed sometimes to be strangling her, especially when the baby's movements inside her were so violent that they woke her at night and she rose to go to the toilet. Ben *always* had his eyes open, it seemed, and he always always asked her when she returned, 'OK?' As if, no banish the stupid thought, he was keeping guard over *his* bump even at night.

He was just a light sleeper, that's all.

Like water dripping on a stone, Ben's little statements about the liberated arrangements they were about to embark on being Every Woman's Dream, came to seem like eternal truths to Margot, and she found her spirits lifting, her confidence growing, her patience and optimism swelling with her insides.

After all everyone kept telling her how lucky she was to have Ben ready and willing, and so involved. Very few fathers, you know, very few, when it comes to the Crunch . . .

So, by the time of the Crunch, that time when the bag is packed for hospital and you watch the calendar and hold your breath and try desperately to concentrate on the television and the radio – in Margot's case two weeks since the baby refused to come on time – she was completely reconciled.

Benny was after all an excellent potential father, she would be able to pursue her career, the sun even shone now and then through the emptying branches of the lime trees on their road.

The nursery was replete with changing station, four mobiles strategically placed over the cot into which Benny had put the smaller carry-cot, so that she would feel cosy. They like to be swaddled tightly like they were in the womb, he told Margot. The posters on all the walls were for 'early visual stimulus', the bucket was for nappies to soak in.

There was nothing he had not thought of. He had even adapted the Kiddy Alert, a device sent from his sister as a present, he explained to Margot, so that he could wear it as earphones, and she could get a full night's sleep.

They waited, in a kind of ecstatic hiatus, completely self-contained and the rest of the world turned colourless and insipid in the radiance of their happiness.

23 *Backtracking*

The only habit which died hard with Ben was walking Geoffrey – he needed to visit the pub some nights. Not for the beer of course since he and Margot bought beer at Sainsbury's with the weekly shopping – but for the company, or so he thought.

At first he kept quiet about his liaison with his lodger, especially since two of his drinking pals were also workmates and had heard about his problems with her. But gradually the truth filtered down to them.

'What's she like then, this teacher?' How could you begin? What they meant was – how *could* you?

They also wanted to know, since Ben had had to inform them of the coming birth and his own prospective role in the child-rearing, how he was going to manage the Woman's Work of looking after the child. Ben had to admit, therefore, that he had been reading books on the subject and even vouchsafed the opinion that child-rearing didn't come naturally to women either – it had to be learnt somehow. Ben wasn't sure whether his anti-sexism or the fact that he had been reading had put the nail in the coffin of his deteriorating relations with his friends, but they certainly began to ignore him so that eventually, several weeks before the birth, he stopped walking Geoffrey altogether.

It was a loss.

Part Three

24 *Resurrection*

There is a rumour that Nature is wonderful. You must let things take their course. Except smallpox and AIDS and famine – you have to draw the line somewhere.

The staff at the Sheffield Maternity Hospital knew where to draw the line. They had not, after all, started the rumour, and in fact only went along with it, providing birthing stools, wallpaper and cassette players in the labour wards, knowing full well that fashion and rumour go hand in hand and go in circles. In a few years they knew they would be revamping with hi-tech aseptic environments to satisfy the next generation of reproducers.

And they drew the line at Margot's baby being fifteen days overdue; they drew it at five o'clock on the evening of the twelfth of October, by telephone, telling her where to come and what to bring.

Then they injected a continuous stream of nature-identical hormones to induce labour and left her and Benny in a side-ward of the Labour Unit to get on with it. To let things take their course.

What they didn't know, because it was no longer thought an acceptable risk to a baby to X-ray an expectant mother, was that Nature had provided Margot with a baby whose head had a greater circumference than the widest opening of the outlet of her pelvis. Isn't Nature wonderful?

So the night shift were surprised when after nine hours very little progress had been made, and mother seemed to be dehydrated (by doing that Infernal Breathing so long) and distressed. The day shift were even more surprised when no further progress had made by noon the next day, despite hours on an epidural, and much sleep. By Margot, Benny was awake the whole time doing what was for him the nearest thing to praying which he could imagine.

*

Ben had by this time made a mental note of the lies they had been told at the ante-natal classes, things like the breathing will reduce the pain and is a Good Idea, music will help keep you calm, first labours often last twelve hours, but never longer.

Benny was sent out when the forceps were attempted. The baby's head was too firmly engaged for a Caesarean to be performed. He was worried. His resolve was slipping for the first time in months. What if the baby were not to survive, or, worse, to survive but brain-damaged, imperfect? He had not thought this was a possibility. It was not in his Plan.

The second attempt at forceps was successful and Benny was called back into the room and handed a bundle. Margot was in a state of sweaty collapse on the table, held by two large nurses.

'It's a girl,' said the nurse as she handed her to him, 'eight pounds exactly.'

Ben had always imagined telling other people that it was a girl, not being told. It didn't matter though. A girl. Of course – he had known all along that it would be a girl.

Benny stood, gazing into her eyes. His own daughter. She was an Ashe completely. His mother's eyes. Deep, deep blue, tawny skin. A little wrinkled. Five toes to each perfect foot, five fingers on each hand, no birthmarks, head only slightly elongated, one nose, two . . .

He was vaguely aware of panic ensuing on the table, of snapped commands, and then of Margot being transferred to a trolley and wheeled away. He looked up. The room was empty but for one nurse standing by him.

'Don't worry, she'll be all right.'

She sounded as if she were lying. Benny did not pursue it. Of course she'll be all right, she's had the baby now. Everything is fine.

'Only,' she wouldn't leave him alone, he turned to walk out of the room, 'the afterbirth won't come away, so they are operating.'

Fortunately in the effort to save Margot's life, everyone forgot Ben so he walked slowly down the corridor to a waiting-room with Baby. He opened his shirt and the front swaddling of her sheet and laid her against his beating heart, and lounged there, his feet resting on the edge of that central swathe of carpet worn bare by pacing fathers, for three hours. Ben knew, from his reading, what vital work he was now doing. Bonding. She was not sleepy (so Jolly was right) but extremely alert and looked deeply into his eyes with hers. He spoke to her with his eyes. Who are you, he asked. Don't you know, she said. Of course I do. I am yours. Right. And we are going to be fine. Very fine. I promise you . . . No, don't make me any promises, we shall just live one day at a time this time. Little Miss Ashe was not only able to see and communicate already, she could also *root*. Thus it was that she discovered Nature's first cruel joke – Daddy's nipples. Ben too felt the cruelty of this idiotic piece of Darwinism for the first time. If only, if only. Sorry about that, said Ben, I have evolved away from you over the centuries, but I promise to make it up to you. No, don't promise me . . . If love as big as the centuries could only . . .

They were interrupted by a nurse who came to tell Ben that Margot was now in Intensive Care and had been given a transfusion and that she would take Baby now. She apologised that he had been left with her so long.

Ben found it hard to understand this grown-up talk or the purport of it at first and then realised that she was stooping to take his baby away from him. He was reluctant until the young nurse explained that they needed to do a few routine tests.

Two hours later Margot awoke in Intensive Care, on her own. She had been dreaming that she was in a very serious car accident and awoke to find it was true for she had a pain as big as a house.

'Not surprising, dear, you've got more stitches in you than the Bayeaux tapestry,' said Mrs Harrison, knitting by her bed. No it wasn't Mrs Harrison on closer inspection. It was also not quite Dorothea. Why did she want to place this person so badly?

Margot also wanted to scream. But she couldn't let herself. In the old days you could scream in the maternity ward, now you must be quiet, polite, consider others. No more screaming.

Where? Where were all the stitches? And how much longer

before she had the baby? Margot felt for her bump and found it had been stolen and screamed after all.

'Hush now! There is no need for that,' said her mother, or Angela or Sally with a mask on. 'I'll bring your baby to you right away.'

The Total Stranger (Margot finally decided) went away and came back wheeling one of those sculptures. The trolley stopped on the right side of the bed, Ben was standing behind it. Margot wanted to lean forward, to see, but she could not, she was held, strapped, pinned down and taped up.

'It's a girl,' said Ben, smiling. 'Well done.'

'I tried to give her some milk but she spat it out. I guess she'd rather have you,' said a nurse, making a clumsy attempt to Promote Bonding, as laid down in the manual.

Margot started to cry. Everyone knew more about her baby than she did.

'There must be some mistake,' she said. 'A girl?'

Ben and the older nurse agreed that Margot should have pain-killers, sleep, and not be bothered with the baby now. This is Intensive Care after all, and the baby did not need any intensive care, only Margot. Ben wheeled the baby away without Margot ever having seen her face.

Every two hours he walked down from the waiting-room, took a bottle out of the fridge and the baby from the IC nursery, to give her a little food.

'If only all fathers were like that,' said a student nurse on duty to the midwife.

'He's in love. It'll pass. Wait for the first nappy,' she said.

'What are you doing?' Benny had sprung in front of the nursery nurse leaning over his daughter's cot.

'Changing her.'

'I'll do that.'

'Will you?'

'Of course. She's mine.'

136

'OK, I take it back. He did it. But how many will he do when she's out of here?'

The younger nurse looked down the corridor, to where Ben was reading, sitting bolt upright, alert, still.

'It doesn't seem quite natural.'

'See, it's your own prejudices, that's all.'

'He doesn't even look worried. His wife's had four pints of blood and he doesn't even ask us how she's doing, and you think I'm prejudiced. There's something wrong here, and I ought to know.'

'Why should he ask, we keep telling him she's fine, don't we?'

When the baby was deeply asleep, Ben phoned Sharon in Australia, and Margot's mother in Bournemouth, and Angela and Andrew at home and, finally, Sally. He had these numbers on a list and felt as if he was going through a ritual, for he was communicating only *facts*.

That night Margot was moved on to an ordinary ward, somewhat unplugged but still heavily sedated, and the baby went with her, to dwell in the small glasshouse of a nursery at the end of the ward with three other babies born that day.

She had regained consciousness in Intensive Care just long enough to hear from the woman in bed next to her how lucky she was not to have *lost* her baby altogether. That woman had lost four babies so far. Margot stopped feeling sorry for herself and vowed that she never would again in her entire life, and then passed out and dreamt again of the same car crash.

At last, there was nothing for it, Ben had to go home, alone. For some reason, possibly that ante-natal preparation classes were actually aimed at mothers rather than fathers, no one had actually told him, and he had been unable to foresee, that he would have to leave his child in a strange building, at the mercy of strangers, and drive home to an empty house. Standing at the car door, unlocking it, it occurred to Ben that this was not a reasonable thing to do; that he should go back, grab her and run. Even when Bet was at her most infuriatingly incontinent, he would not have considered putting her in One of Those Places.

*

However he must above all not do anything to jeopardise the future. And a little patience now would pay off later. He was permitted to come again at seven-thirty the following morning, and at seven twenty-five he would be waiting outside the electric doors.

On the way home great happiness and great tiredness fell upon him. The two states mounted their steeds and took up arms to charge at each other.

It was almost eleven o'clock when Ben parked in front of his house, but he had to tell someone. He decided to make Mrs Harrison's day, and knocked loudly on her door. She answered it far too swiftly in her dressing-gown. She must have heard him drive up.

'Well?' she asked, almost smiling, the flabby folds of her face trembling wildly.

'A girl. Eight pounds exactly!' shouted Benny, and gave her a big hug. She seemed to stagger and laugh a little, but was not apparently put out by his sudden passion.

'And the mother?'

Benny paused for a minute, he had almost forgotten Margot.

'She had a bit of a hard time.'

'Caesarean, was it?'

'Partly, and partly forceps. She's all right now.'

Mrs Harrison congratulated him, and hurried off to bed. She would have a busy day tomorrow, telling at least twenty-seven people as many details as she could invent between now and then on the meagre information Benny had given her.

Tiredness admitted defeat and Benny, no longer the future Prime Minister, but, far more importantly, Future Father of the Century and his champion, Happiness, entered the house.

25 *Despatch Box*

Ben's happiness evaporated the moment he let himself into the hall of the house.

'That you, Benny?' It was Mother.

Ben shut the door, his hand shaking, and made as if to kick Geoffrey against the bottom of the door, but it had gone. He ran down the dark hall to the door to her room which was locked.

'Mother, where are you?'

He found the key in his pocket and used it. The room was black. She had not even turned on the light. Typical! He switched it on. Nothing: he had removed the bulb. She is not there, not anywhere. He strained with his ears until his cheeks hurt.

'Mother!' he called. 'I have got such news.' What news?

There is never a right time to marry, to have a baby, to grieve. But Benny is committed now, with the birth of his daughter, into the flux of time, and it swept him up in the middle of his ecstasy and dropped him into the eye of the storm of grief which has waited ten months and will not wait one more moment.,

Oh not *now*, weeps Benny, falling into a sitting position by the wall under the high window through which fall beams of darkness streaked with darkness.

I have got such news. He struggles to keep hold of his news. Like the ten-year-old, cap askew, with grey shorts running home with his 11-plus results to find Sharon feverish with scarlet fever and he is ignored. He went to sleep on the sofa that night hearing the sinister flap-flapping of the wet carbolic sheet over the door to their bedroom with the News still clutched in his hand.

'I'll hear thy news, lad,' said his father bending over him, through the cloud of tobacco smoke. No, I've no news now.

And was I once skin on skin to his beating heart and I wouldn't tell him my news? No, never. Not then, in those days. He was at work when I was born. Heard of it by report. It was enough in those days. Who says it was enough? It was all there was, but it may not have been enough. He may have longed for something more, in his heart, he may have . . . Ben howls now, howls and

139

howls, not for his father or his mother or all the people he has no news for, but for himself and his evil plan.

Just yesterday he read that if a tree falls in a forest and there is no ear to hear it, it perhaps makes no sound falling. He had laughed. If philosophers were initiated into the ins and outs of television repair they would understand properly what a sound wave was, how measurable, how *real*, he had thought. But now the truth of it, the sadness of it, came to him. The birth of his child is just a tree falling in a world devoid of ears, a piece of news on a piece of paper which a small boy clutched and clutched and then lost in the night. If Bet is not available for the news, there is no news.

His heavy shadow interrupts the beams of darkness from the window thick like the perfumes of heady summer in a hedgerow; the air is full of dark down too solid to breathe. But he was able, finally, to cry, and in that, there was some purpose, some possibility of change.

The last time Ben had cried had been just as unexpected. Coming home from a night away (why?) he entered the front room, then the parlour, where his mother had just finished giving a piano lesson to a large girl from down the road. He ran over to her and sat on her lap. She said, 'You're too big a boy to sit on my lap any more,' and hugged him as if she were going away. 'I hope I die before you,' Benny had said and she stood up, dropping him onto the floor. 'NO!' she had shouted, 'No, silly boy, that's whole point of having thee and Sharon, to go on after. You've both to survive us a long, long time.' 'But I don't want to,' and he cried and cried, his tears falling on the row of yellow and black keys and dripping between the keys to disappear – trying to imagine the unimaginable: a world without Mother.

Ben sat on the brittle old linoleum, curled at the joins, with nothing in his hands, in the empty room, seeing nothing. The past is cancelled. There is no one to hear his news, no one to interpret it, so the world is without meaning, without Bet.

26 *Betrayal*

The next morning Ben arrived in the ward to find that his daughter had betrayed him. First of all, she was not waiting for him in her plastic cabin on wheels in the nursery. He walked into the ward.

Margot was sitting up supported by dozens of pillows with one on her lap. Across this pillow lay Baby sucking furiously at the outsize breast dangling over her head. Margot was smiling, and looked up the moment he entered, her eyes full of love.

Ben tried, and almost failed, to smile.

'Look,' she said, 'at least there's one thing I can do right, and all on my own.' Then she added, 'You look awful.'

'I wasn't able to sleep,' he replied.

Ben sat, stroking Baby's head, having kissed Margot silently on the forehead, and listened to her babble. She told him of the controversy over the breastfeeding. One midwife had told her people who had had Caesareans could not breastfeed, another had said that was rubbish, the doctor had said she must not be exhausted by the baby's demands, another doctor had said breastfeeding would promote healing, and she must try it. Finally she had given up on them all and asked the woman in the bed next to her who had opined that the baby had *not* been born by Caesarean, only the afterbirth, and who was allowed to get out and walk around to go get the baby for her. Ever since then she had been feeding her happily, making it up as she went along . . .

Ben decided to accept it gracefully, and encouraged her by telling her that what she was giving her now wasn't milk but colostrum which was vital for her immune system, and to keep it up, at least while she was in hospital. Obviously she couldn't feed her when she was at work, so it was better to give her the best while she could.

Of course, now that Margot was awake and alert, she had noticed Ben looking into the nursery window, and his crestfallen face when he saw her breastfeeding. Angela had warned her about this, and she was rather pleased to see Ben exhibiting a Normal Male Reaction. Angela had explained it thus: your breasts 'belong' to your lover, your man, he sees them as elements of his desire and affection for you. And there you are offering them to another, even though it is his own child. He is bound to feel jealous at first. He has just got to do a lot of growing up quite suddenly. This was certainly true of Benny – after all he had until quite recently been a Mother's Boy himself, and was only just hovering on the verge of becoming literate in a way.

Sally, had she been there, could have pointed out two faults in this argument; one that the baby was a girl and not a boy (as Angela's was) and so the jealousy factor was straining credibility a bit, even on a Freudian level; and two, that Ben had reacted very positively to his first sight of breastfeeding. Common sense, too, if it had been there might have pointed out that since it was so long since Ben and Margot had made love, he was hardly likely to remember her breasts, let alone feel possessive about them. Still, it was one of those good and handy theories that slotted nicely into the moment like a favourite woolly pullover you remembered to bring on a camping trip which turns chilly.

'And fortunately you are such an expert on the subject, I shall have all the advice I need,' she added, smiling at him. Benny now experienced that feeling which Margot had once felt that he was with someone he didn't know. She wanted, suddenly, to make him feel important, involved. He hoped she wasn't going to become, contrary to all his expectations, a Wonderful Person, after all.

Released from the breast, the baby started waving her arms and legs about quite wildly.

'Busy bee,' said Ben, taking her in his arms while Margot reinstated her breast into a piece of equipment she must have secretly provided herself with: a gigantic Feeding Bra. It had dozens of hook-and-eye fasteners down the front and took her a few minutes to fasten. Also it was the wrong design, for it provided no support for the breast not in use. If only she had consulted him, he would never have let her buy this one.

'Funny you should say that, I've decided I want to call her Bea, Beatrice I mean. What do you think?'

'No,' said Ben, without looking up. Margot was surprised. They had not discussed names beforehand because they wanted to see what she was like first, rather than arbitrarily impose a name on someone they had not yet met.

142

'Why not?'

'If you are thinking of Dante,' he said (Margot's mouth involuntarily fell open at this), 'I don't like the idea. She was simply the object of a pederast's desire.'

'Oh.'

'Elizabeth,' he said, taking off a nappy, and slipping a new one under her bottom from the tray beneath the plastic cabin at his side.

Margot played with the name.

'Lizzie, Izzie, Betty, Lizziebet, Eliza. Lots of possibilities, I agree, but don't you think it's a bit Monarchist?'

'What you got against the Queen, then?'

'Oh, nothing.'

'Mother of four.'

'True. Probably breastfed them all.'

'No, hardly, I think.'

'Who would have stopped her?'

'Public opinion.'

Before he left, Benny felt he had re-established contact with Elizabeth and came back from the nursery to say goodbye to Margot, who was settling down to sleep. She asked him to do her a favour. At first she seemed afraid to ask him. He had to guess what it was. I've phoned your mother, he said, what else could it be?

She pulled down the sheet and pulled up her nightdress, closing her eyes.

'I can't bear to look. Will you tell me what it looks like?' she asked.

Above the line of her pants there was a ten-inch, red gash held together with a row of metal clips, not unlike the fasteners on her bra. Benny found himself sucking in his breath. All at once he realised what she had gone through, and would go through. He delved into an almost lost self where he had invented the leaking hot-water bottles for Bet.

'Oh, it's nothing,' he said, 'looks like a little appendix scar to me. About four stitches, no more. I think it's what they call the bikini line. It won't even show in a few weeks.'

'Oh, good. It feels like I've been cut in half.'

'Ask them for painkillers. They'll give you.'

'They do. Every few hours a trolley comes round and they give us something called a Cocktail, which the lady in the next bed says is morphine.'

It passed through his mind that if she was taking morphine, so was Elizabeth, which might be his best argument against breast-feeding, but he let it pass.

'Well, don't get hooked. I'd have to turn to crime to keep you in morphine on the outside.' She laughed. Ben covered the scar up, and breathed normally again.

But that red gash through which Elizabeth had not entered the world haunted him over the next ten days. Subject as he was to frequent nightmares during those first long, lonely nights in the empty house, that gash ran from one of her star-and-moon earrings to the other, across her throat, and not only was he responsible for the injury, and wanted by the police, but he had also to remove the clips himself, without her realising, while she slept. Just as he reached for the first clip, she opened her eyes, and, terrified, he felt himself falling and awoke.

27 *Fraternising*

On the second whole day of new Elizabeth's life Ben again spent a large part of the day in the hospital, changed two nappies, watched Margot proudly displaying her newly allowed mobility: she could swing her legs onto a bedside chair, hobble down and walk across to the toilet very, very slowly. This is someone who went skiing most winters, jogging some mornings, he mused. But all the other women in the ward walked like this, though some a little faster, presumably because they were day three or four. Without exception they had to climb down the four feet from their beds by means of the unsteady chairs by the side of them. Why on earth, thought Ben, don't they install beds which go up and down, like a dentist's chair. They do, said the woman in the next bed to Margot, for the private patients.

Was there ever, ever, thought Benny, really a time when women squatted behind a bush, gave birth, and went back to work in the fields? Surely not, not really.

He was revising his thoughts on the inequality of evolution a little as he watched these women, debilitated, tearful, fragile, vulnerable – you certainly couldn't have everyone reproducing under these circumstances. Someone has got to be fit. Someone has to keep marauders at bay, spear the odd buffalo.

By the time Margot had returned, scaled again single-handedly the four feet up to her bed (no, don't help me, I have to get strong), and arranged herself on the rubber tyre, she looked as exhausted as someone who had just run a marathon.

'Hand me the hairbrush, Ben, I must look a sight,' she murmured.

'No, you're fine,' he said, and ran his free hand, the one which was not holding Elizabeth, up over her forehead and through her hair. She closed her eyes and seemed about to sleep.

'Your mother is coming tomorrow. Tell me what she's like.'

Margot opened one eye and closed it again, groaning. 'She used to be unbearably manipulative and repulsive, now she is unbearably kind and Christian and doubly repulsive.'

Ben laughed. 'So, you reckon I'll take to her, then?'

'Oh yes, you'll love her. You could do me the favour of murdering her – we'd stand to inherit a fortune *and* rid the world of a nuisance.'

Ben laughed, and laughed. Margot stopped him.

'It's not that funny.'

'It is. It is. Really I meant what does she look like. She seemed to assume I'd know her at the station. I suppose she thought I'd seen photographs.'

After a pause during which Ben thought she might have fallen asleep, she said, 'Well she looks like me only much fatter, with purple-grey hair, blue winged glasses and tweedy clothes. Oh, and she always wears lace-ups now she's a Christian, and a rather ostentatious cross.'

'Ostentatious . . .,' said Ben to Elizabeth, 'that's the sort of word we'll soon be teaching you. None of that down-to-earth four-letter stuff, none of that "Dada", "Mama", "doggy" stuff, but good big words like Ostentatious: or Capacious or Rampatious . . .'

Margot laughed. 'What did you say?'

'I wasn't talking to you.'

'Oh, that's how it's going to be, is it?'

Thus there grew up a kind of bantering while Margot was as

firmly pinned to her hospital bed as dead moths to the polystyrene which gave Ben a sense of security as of a comfort object, and made Margot more hopeful about the future. She always knew he would change the nappies but she never dared to hope he would jolly her along like this.

Ben felt at home when hand in hand with someone struggling along the unknown parameters of existence – birth and death. Margot's brush with death had endeared her to him, at least for the time being, and his love for Elizabeth was overwhelming his rational self.

28 *Reinforcements*

On the third day of Elizabeth's life, her only living grandparent came to visit. Since she had come so far, she arranged to stay with Benny. Ben was apprehensive about this since all he knew about her was that she was wealthy and 'into Jesus in a big way'. Neither of these characteristics predicted that they would coexist at all happily. Also, he had hoped to avoid ever having to meet her, though he realized now how foolish this hope had been.

He met her at the station, recognising her by the purple hair and lace-ups (congratulating himself on not having had to look up ostentatious or admit to ignorance of it), and was dismayed that she carried with her a very large suitcase. He hoped it was entirely stuffed with presents for the baby rather than the means to stay in Sheffield for weeks.

Ben soon decided that the best stance for him to adopt was one of mysterious silence, since this would give him time to assess her and thus the advantage over her. Like Margot, she seemed determined to tell him everything about herself and more before they had even arrived at the hospital, which he had decided would be their first port of call. After all, he wanted to make it clear to her that this was the main and only point of her visit, to see Elizabeth and Margot, and nothing else.

So during that car ride Mrs Mason informed Ben that he was better looking than she had expected, that this baby was an answer to her prayers (and he had thought having sex with
146

Margot had done it!), that if they should need any financial assistance while Margot was on half pay during maternity leave, he was to apply to her, that they were all three welcome to spend every summer holiday at Bournemouth, where the air was better than here, the people friendlier and more talkative, but she expected he was a shy person, she was in fact a shy person herself. Also she said that she could only stay three days since she had agreed to help with a camp for deprived London children who were having a Christian weekend in Bournemouth. She could tell he was disappointed by his face, but she was sorry, she was committed. Committed to Christ, she meant. Was he? No. Well, she rather suspected that being a parent things might suddenly appear in a different light, you never know. Is this the hospital, gosh what a drab place, she wasn't used to the North, everything is so . . .

Ben took her to the nursery window first and asked her to guess. Go on, he said, you ought to be able to recognise her.

Mrs Mason wandered between the four cabins. She chose one. Ben laughed. She looked closely at his face again, and chose another. Then she read the name on the wristband.

'It's not fair,' she said, 'she doesn't look a bit like Margot. Or like you quite. I'm not sure . . .'

'She is the spitting image of my mother,' said Ben, grabbing the edge of the trolley to wheel it into the ward. 'Come on, let's wake Margot.'

Margot's mother wept, hugging her daughter.

'Mind my stitches, Mum,' was all Margot said and raised her eyebrows to Ben over the purple-rinsed locks.

Ben pulled her away, slotted an arm round Margot's shoulders and pulled her clear, adjusting the metal bedpost and pillows with the free hand most professionally, to make her upright enough to receive Elizabeth.

'Oh, how clever, you're not a nurse, are you?' asked Margot's mother.

'Hasn't Margot told you what I am?' Ben asked, easing Elizabeth down onto the covers, for inspection.

'No, she never tells me anything.'

'You never asked me,' said Margot, bitterly.

147

'I don't like to pry. What do you do, Benedict?'

'I am an unemployed philosopher,' he said. Margot hid her giggles behind a hand. 'Aren't I, Margot?'

'Definitely.'

But Margot's mother was in another world, unpacking her one and only grandchild from the hospital swaddling. At first she prayed inwardly, thanking Him for the perfection of this little person, for the sheer joy she felt gazing at the bundle of life. Like Ben she counted everything, hunted for unsightly birthmarks, stork-marks, strawberry marks, moles, missing earlobes and so on.

Then, as Margot related, without euphemism (for her own reasons she did not wish to spare her mother any of the gruesomeness of it), a blow by blow account of Elizabeth's entry into the world and her own subsequent emergencies, the internal praying died down a little. Until by the end, so rapt was she that she let her eyes leave the baby (Ben re-wrapped her and rolled her towards him) and looked only at Margot's swollen, tear-stained face. Blowing her nose, she almost heard that still, small voice cry out, 'How could you?' for any hurt to your own child is a hurt to you but stilled it, and hugged Margot again.

'His ways are mysterious, Margot,' she said, blowing her nose again.

'Let's do Him the favour of supposing He had nothing to do with it, Mum.'

The unemployed philosopher got on with the nappy, grinning at his daughter, who nearly grinned back, though they say it is only wind makes babies so philosophical.

During the journey home Ben prepared himself for the worst three days of his life, but he was to be pleasantly surprised. First of all she sat during the ride in a silence so complete that he felt embarrassed into talking, and found himself telling her all about the alterations they had undertaken to the house, which she seemed to be listening attentively to. On the other hand perhaps she hadn't really heard because the only thing she said the whole journey was, 'No one in my family ever had that much trouble — did your mother perhaps . . . ?'

'My sister and I were born at home,' said Ben, 'here in fact.'

*

On entering the house she pronounced it 'charming' and wandered round approving of everything. Except the contents of the fridge and food cupboards which abounded with wholefood, sesame seeds, retexturised protein nodules, wobbly slabs of milk-white tofu in dishes of cloudy water, jars of damp seeds so old they were sprouting where they lay.

'They are meant to sprout,' said Ben. 'Margot loves them.'

'Well I don't know where she got that from. I brought her up on proper meat and two vegetables.'

She declared that Ben needed building up, and a trip to Marks and Spencer's food hall was in order. Ben said he never shopped there. He boycotted M&S, but he couldn't remember why. (Sally had told him to; it was something to do with their policy on breastfeeding on the premises.) She insisted he call her Dorothy, and they went shopping. Dorothy simply put on her coat, picked up an empty PVC shopping bag and handed him his car keys.

They went where she wanted to go, and she paid for everything.

First they bought an enormous quantity of expensive (some pre-cooked) food in M&S (Ben kept his flat cap pulled down over his eyes so that no one he knew would spot him). Then, dumping this in the car, they went to Mothercare and practically denuded the shop of its stock. Though Ben had done well, he had not 'thought ahead' enough, she declared. There were pushchairs to buy, swinging devices which fitted onto door frames, walking frames, all of which could be stored away until needed. She also bought second copies of some things he had already bought – you need *two* changing mats she told him, one for the upstairs bathroom, one for the kitchen downstairs. He would also need more toys, she told him. Babies get bored with just a few. Also she bought four night-dresses with a special front opening for Margot. So a strange mixture of bright plastic things, linen and hardware went into the trolley and they staggered back to the car.

They called into the Off Licence on the way home, just for a couple of bottles. To celebrate. Ben expected her to buy champagne or wine. She bought one two-quart bottle of whisky and a smaller one of gin. Also two bottles of tonic water. The quinine is so good for one.

*

That evening they spent drinking until they were both leglessly drunk, unpacking the items bought and after a few rousing choruses from 'Onward Christian Soldiers', to which Ben was able to introduce Dorothy to a completely new set of words, much to her delight, they went to their beds more or less on all fours.

The next morning he found Mrs Harrison sitting in his own kitchen, opposite Dorothy, drinking tea. He was so astounded, he stood with his mouth open, hoping some Alka Seltzer would fall into it from the ceiling.

'I've cooked you bacon and eggs, it's in the oven, dear,' said Dorothy, 'and Mrs Harrison has kindly called in to ask after Margot and the baby. We're just having a lovely chat . . .'

Ben sat and ate his breakfast while they continued chatting. Mrs Harrison hardly had a chance to utter a word but he could tell that like him she was able to take notes in her head, and was taking it all down for future reference.

It was only when Dorothy mentioned that the baby looked like Ben's mother that he was unable to go on chewing. His heart beat so fast he thought he would be sick.

'Did you know Mrs Ashe, then?' asked Mrs Harrison, quite reasonably, looking at Benny, who looked down at his food quickly.

'No, of course not. In any case, she is such a pretty little thing, you'll be amazed Mrs Harrison when . . .'

Before she left Mrs Harrison made so bold as to ask Benny a direct question.

Were they naming her Elizabeth, then, she wanted to know. Yes, Ben said, we are. In honour of my mother.

'Lovely. I think that's a lovely idea,' said Dorothy, pouring him another cup of real coffee. 'In fact Margot, Margueritte that is, is named for my mother . . .'

Before lunch they visited Margot and Elizabeth and the night-dresses were received with much exclamation by Margot who was moved to tears by her mother's generosity. In fact everything seemed to be moving her to tears. Ben told her how he and Dorothy had bought up Mothercare and gone home and got pissed, hoping to amuse her. Instead she burst out crying.

'Well we were only celebrating,' he began.

She not only wept the whole visit, she accused them of wasting money, not loving her, conspiring against her, keeping the baby from her (she's just sleeping, I'll get her for you, darling, if . . .), not caring, not enquiring after her stitches, after her sore breasts, her vulval stitches ('Well!' said Dorothy to this), and of a few hundred other crimes.

'It's day three,' said Dorothy, whispering to Ben, 'you always get weepy on day . . .'

'Why are you whispering? What are you hatching?' Margot asked, between sobs. Ben handed her the box of tissues from the bedside cabinet, and said nothing.

There was a pause during which Margot blew her nose. Ben was inventing a complicated joke about saving her moisture for milk production when she turned to him and almost shouted: 'AND HE RAPED ME! THAT'S HOW SHE WAS CONCEIVED!' Everyone in the ward, patients, nurses, fathers visiting, people mopping the floor and wheeling trolleys with tea on them, stopped and looked towards Margot's bed.

Ben froze, staring at the window behind her.

'Now, Margot, don't be silly, dear,' began Dorothy, moving towards her.

'AND YOU KEEP AWAY FROM ME YOU HYPOCRITICAL JESUS FREAK, YOU CHRISTIAN FASCIST, YOU, YOU, YOU POOR EXCUSE FOR A MOTHER!'

At this point a senior nurse strode down the ward with two nurses in tow and a small box.

'Now, now, Mrs Ashe,' began the senior nurse.

'I AM *NOT* MRS ASHE,' shouted Margot, 'I AM NOT MRS ANYTHING. This man is nothing to me, just someone who got me drunk . . .'

They had turned her and injected a hefty dose of sedative into her right buttock before she could continue the story, all true of course, which nearly everyone there knew to be the fevered imaginings of someone dangerously near the beginning of post-natal depression in its severest form, and at the mercy of the hormones Nature had kindly flooded her with to help with milk production.

Margot slept. While she slept Dorothy took Ben out to lunch to 'cheer him up' and Elizabeth was so hungry and cried so loudly, even though the nursing staff offered her water, that they had to give her two small bottles of baby formula. The senior nursing officer wrote a few sentences in Margot's notes which were about as fair and accurate, in cosmic terms, as those bitter little comments Margot used to write about her difficult students, knowing that the students themselves would never read them.

Over lunch Dorothy waxed philosophical about babies, motherhood, hormones, fatherhood, and sex.

Ben was fascinated to discover, now being tuned in to her euphemistic turn of phrase, that to women all Thing is rape, in a sense, since they do not really enjoy Thing as such, only as an expression of someThing else. She did not say of what else. Of course men do not realise this, and it is just as well that they don't because they are, as you know, more sensitive than they are usually given credit for: and most men would not happily go on having Thing with someone if they thought they did not reciprocate the enjoyment. Then where would the Human Race be? Hence there was a certain amount of 'dissemination' which has to go on. Ben asked her to say what kind of dissemination (which he was half sure was something to do with semen) she meant, not wanting, since he had cast himself as a philosopher, to ask the meaning of the word. Oh just a harmless sort of acting, she replied. You get my drift? He got her drift.

But it didn't seem to be a drift which had anything to do with Margot, though if it helped to explain her outburst in the hospital he was happy to let it appear so.

Dorothy then went on to say that she thought she might be able to stay an extra day. Was this part of the drift? What about the Christian Weekend, asked Ben. She thought they could do without her this once. Ben didn't like to say he also felt that way. So she stayed an extra day, long enough to be apologised to by Margot, and long enough to be allowed to feed Elizabeth a bottle, since she was now on half bottle and half breast which the nursing staff felt suited her enormous appetite better. She also gave Ben a passbook for an account she had opened for Elizabeth (it contained four hundred pounds) before she left.

Drift. Ben thought Margot drifted a lot now. For the rest of her stay in hospital she seemed always to be drifting in and out of sleep, and hardly a whole conversation could pass between them without her drifting off to sleep.

Ben did once ask Sister if it were really necessary now to give her quite so many drugs. You'll have to speak to the doctor about that, she said, it's not up to me. Ben never saw a doctor, so he never had the chance. In any case, he wouldn't have *dared*.

There was still in him, despite his dealings with his mother's doctor, an uneasiness about men in white coats. He still felt they lived in some other, more rarified, world – the world of science perhaps which, despite all his reading, was to him a closed book. So he watched Margot languish in the bed when she ought to have been interacting with Elizabeth.

29 *Sabotage*

Though by day Margot was learning to be a mother, the nights belonged to Ben.

Once she was home he systematically sabotaged the half-and-half rhythm which the hospital had helped Margot to impose on little Elizabeth, a rhythm of four-hourly breastfeeds alternated by four-hourly bottles, followed by a night composed largely of unconsciousness and only two short feeds.

This routine did not suit Ben, the Prime Caretaker-to-be. He woke little Elizabeth every two hours in the night, fed her from a bottle, and played with her to keep her awake. Gradually she became tired in the day, and slept for long periods, feeding largely at night. She was at her most active during the nights, the nights which belonged to Ben.

The midwife came every day and on the fifth day home, the fifteenth of the baby's life, Margot complained of the pain and swelling in her breasts and the fact that the baby seemed too tired to suck for long. The milk seemed to be building up, undrunk.

*

Worried, the midwife weighed her. She had already put on several ounces. There was no need to worry. Ben put forward the idea that Elizabeth preferred the bottle. Well they do, agreed the midwife, because it's easier to suck. Perhaps, she also suggested, and this suggestion was like a dagger through Margot's heart, perhaps Mother's milk was a bit thin, a bit insubstantial. Perhaps it would be better all round to give it up now.

'Rubbish! Absolute crap!' said Sally later that day – finally allowed to visit. 'Mother's milk can't be thin, or insubstantial, and no baby in the universe would prefer that manufactured muck. The woman doesn't know what she's talking about. She probably failed to breastfeed her own forty years ago and wants every other woman under her care to fail as well, to make her feel better.'

Sally was only trying to reassure Margot, and standing up for her right to know what was best for her own baby, but Margot was not about to use her as a role model, so Ben smiled tolerantly at them both. Angela came later and was also bottle feeding now. Sally left, feeling defeated. What was wrong with all these women?

After she had left they all agreed that midwives of thirty years' experience couldn't be wrong about such a simple thing and somehow, despite Margot's tears, it was agreed that Elizabeth should go on the bottle.

After all, Margot, you wouldn't want to be still feeding the baby at a year and a half, like she is. Andrew made a quip about 'feeding through the school railings'.

Margot felt, deep, deep inside her, that she was being deprived of something, but she could not say what. Of the necessity of getting up periodically thus interrupting her sleep, of having to expose her breasts at inconvenient moments? Surely she was only giving up a set of chains she would have to shake off when she returned to work anyway?

Ben would have preferred Elizabeth to be breast fed. After all it was best for baby, and all Sally's arguments seemed more than reasonable to him, but it was a sacrifice he had to make.

*

One piece of good advice the midwife did give was that Margot should have a nap in the afternoon whether or not Baby did. This she did religiously, between one-thirty and four o'clock every day.

On the fifth of November Ben tucked Elizabeth into the Babypak on his front and set off for the park. It was bitterly cold and he regretted taking her out of the house. He kept pulling back her head to check she was not blue.

It seemed as if the whole of Sheffield had taken the opportunity to rid themselves of unwanted furniture, trees, sheds, and so on, for the pile in the middle of the field was about a hundred feet high and sixty feet wide at the bottom. Children were gathering sticks to poke around under it in case any hedgehogs were trapped.

'Hello! Ben!' It was Sally with Enoch in his pushchair, just coming round the pile towards him.

'Why is it always freezing cold on November 5th?'

Since Margot would still be asleep, Ben invited Sally to come home with him and have some tea.

It was three o'clock on a cold autumn afternoon. She watched him making up the formula, shaking it, testing it on the inside of his bare elbow. She looked down at the little moon face of Elizabeth in her arms and shifted her weight on the kitchen stool.

'Ben, you did it deliberately, didn't you?'

He tried to take the baby from her; she resisted, pulling her up to her chin.

'Let me feed her, just a little.'

'NO! Your milk is all wrong for her.'

'Why? It's better than that stuff. Go on. Let me.'

He took Elizabeth by force and walked over to the window. The shadow of Mrs Harrison moved away across the passage.

'Because I'm black, is it?'

'No! God, no, I don't mean that. Only Enoch is eleven months, so your milk is different. It changes.'

'Does it?'

She watched him angling the bottle, settling the baby against him tightly.

155

'But if you know so much about it, how could you . . . ?'
Enoch had toddled out of sight and she ran down the hall to
catch him. He was just pulling himself upright by the telephone
cable.
'That's amazing,' said Ben, 'he walks already.'
'He's been walking since seven months,' said Sally.
'Why so early?'
'Black babies do,' she laughed, 'but let's not compete. Elizabeth
won't walk so early.'

They went into the sitting-room, more toddler-proof than the
kitchen, and sat on the sofa, quite close.
'You must have known,' she pursued. Ben only smiled at her.
She asked him why, softened now, beginning to accept it.
Somehow the sight of him cradling the baby, feeding it, how-
soever by bottle, the lovingness of it moved her. He said he
thought she could work it out for herself and she said that
although she thought she could understand, she also thought it
was a despicable thing to do, supposing that he wanted absolute
control, absolute power over the child. Ben felt he needed to
defend himself and told her that he had asked Margot if she and
Enoch could have the flat and she had vetoed it.
Sally stood up angrily.
'You shouldn't have told me that,' she said. 'You ought to be
more loyal and it's got nothing to do with it.'
Ben helped her manoeuvre the pushchair down their stone
steps at the front of the house. Sally had timed her exit so that
Margot would not know they had been, and Ben did not tell her,
though by Sally's rules he should have, out of loyalty.

And he should have all the other times to come, when she and
Enoch would happen to be passing and drop in at this time.

Ben finally paid the price of shifting Elizabeth from breast to
bottle that night. For Margot developed mastitis of both breasts
and was in agony, and it was a Sunday and no doctor could
come till the evening. She cried with the pain, could not lie
down, could not bear the sound of Elizabeth crying, or even of
Ben boiling the kettle. Even the bangs and whizzes of the first
early fireworks fired her nerves. Mrs Harrison rang the doorbell
156

and asked whether she could help, and received abuse from Ben. Ben phoned Sally who advised very hot towels and ice cubes alternately over each breast and offered to come over. He would not let her. He thought the sight of Sally at such a time might unhinge Margot completely.

Ben sat at the end of the bed, having fed and changed Elizabeth and put her to sleep in another room, with a dozen pamphlets spread out before him.

'I am dying and you are reading pamphlets!' wailed Margot.

'That must be the Raving Monster in me then,' he said, not pausing in his research, 'and you are not dying.'

'I wish I was. You enjoy watching me suffer!'

'I'm not watching you. I am trying to read. Will you please shut up, or moan quietly to yourself.'

Margot threw off the cooling wet towels and turned into the pillow, sure that her swollen breasts would set fire to the bed and burn the house down.

For surely her milk had turned to gunpowder. Ben's head came close to hers and he asked her, in a whisper, as if someone might overhear them, 'Margot, have you got a vibrator?'

She whipped round in the bed, furious. 'A *what*? You're mad. Now I know it, completely *mad*! Owwwwwwww!'

Ben went into the bathroom and started looking for things as noisily as possible. After enough crashing to wake the dead, he came back with an electric shaver and unplugged her clock radio by the bed.

'Sit up,' he ordered her, holding the buzzing razor in one hand. 'Sit up, Margot!' She sat.

'What are you going to do?' She had some idea that the machine would remove her breasts entirely (not such a bad idea, passed through her mind, much as someone with a migraine headache contemplates decapitation with some pleasure).

'Since we are not, obviously, a Modern Liberated Couple with Marital Aids, we shall have to improvise.' Now she thought he had some really kinky intention and her eyes widened.

'Perhaps we should wait for the doctor after all,' she said. 'This is just an idea from a book, isn't it? How do you know . . .'

'And aren't all your ideas out of books, Miss? Don't you make a living out of ideas out of books?'

She closed her eyes, like one on the guillotine, and said, 'Do it.'

He moved the trembling machine downwards over each breast from shoulder to nipple, from rib to nipple, from armpit to nipple, and after ten minutes Margot began to see the point, or rather to feel the benefit. The blockages which Elizabeth had not been allowed to clear the natural way were being vibrated along the ducts and out by means of the electric vibration of this shaver.

'Oh, brilliant, Ben, brilliant,' she said. 'Sorry, I take back everything I said.'

'Oh don't do that,' said Ben, 'I love it when you're angry.'

Margot frowned at him, 'What *have* you been reading?'

'Words, words, words . . .'

Drifting off into sleep, she asked drowsily whether that was a quotation she ought to recognise. Ben phoned Sally to say the crisis was over and took the phone off the hook. The doctor came at nine and prescribed antibiotics and insisted on explaining to Ben how to bandage the breasts tightly when she was next awake.

Ben could have worked it out for himself but his odd sense of humour was touched upon watching this strange young doctor in the chill of the open front doorway making a kind of rotated benediction over his own chest. 'Criss-cross the bandage like this.' Thank you for the blessing, Ben thought, laughing inside that one young man was giving another young man some ancient female wisdom as the explosions of Guy Fawkes lit up the sky behind him.

'She's fine now, Mrs Harrison; and I'm sorry I swore at thee' – a dark scuffling rattled behind the door next-door.

The midwife the following day listened to Margot's story and nodded wisely; this confirmed her original theory that the milk was not good and had 'curdled' (to put it in lay terms) inside the breast. Thank goodness they had changed over to the bottle. Sally opined (and Ben knew every word was true) that giving up the breastfeeding had *caused* the mastitis, caused a congestion and she should have let Elizabeth clear the ducts.

No matter. Elizabeth thrived, and was soon pronounced to be a Daddy's girl. Ben's confusion deepened as the weeks went on. Sally came while Margot slept and one day accused him of not loving Margot at all, and being the Ultimate Male Chauvinist rather than the Liberated Man he was masquerading as. During the discussion that followed, he regretted telling her that she need not come again. He felt as if he had lost his greatest ally. And he was short enough of friends now to feel it.

When Margot was fit enough to walk about, she thought she would prune the garden, so that they could stand the pram in the sunshine. Even though it was mid November, Baby needed some fresh air. The south side – the little front area was too steep.

Charlie sent the boys to assist one day with a pickup truck, removing much of the debris which was not nature's doing. Standing by the wall watching them with great satisfaction, Margot started at a voice near her left ear. It was Mrs Harrison, who commented on how friendly she had found Margot's mother to be, and how pretty the baby looked *from a distance* and to be sure to put her feet up in the afternoons. Bringing Elizabeth closer for a real inspection, Margot replied that she always had a nap between two and four and Mrs Harrison nodded loosely, adding what a shame that she must then miss her black visitor who always came at that time of the day. Oh, who do you mean? The young girl with the toddler. Pretty young thing. Very black though (in a whisper). Oh you mean Sally, yes she's a great friend of mine, said Margot.

Mrs Harrison knew better. Great friend indeed. Great friends don't visit you when you're asleep. The goings on. Good thing Mrs Ashe was no longer here to see.

That day Margot only 'napped' for half an hour and, having set the clock, crept back downstairs to find Ben with Elizabeth strapped into the pram, continuing her work in the garden. There was no Sally about. She sat on a deckchair watching and

159

no one came or even phoned. Mrs Harrison must have been stirring up trouble. Perhaps she did once come, just *once*? If so, why had Ben kept it a secret?

Later Margot made a meal, much to Ben's annoyance (well, you were busy in the garden) and asked him if Sally ever came when she was asleep. He admitted that she had, only to see Elizabeth and he more or less promised that she would not be a regular visitor once Margot was back at work. Then Margot relented, after three glasses of wine, and said what right had she to say what visitors he could have, it wasn't reasonable, and he shouldn't have to live like a recluse with the baby. In fact, she didn't know what had made her say it.

'Jealousy, I expect.'

'Oh, is there any need for me to be jealous, then?'

'I don't think there is ever any need for anyone to be jealous; it is simply a useless and destructive emotion.' Ben was pleased with his answer, since he was beginning to extract his own opinions from the various Guides he had read to Psychology, Philosophy, Literature, etc. The Othello example had so often been quoted that he had actually sat down and read the play one afternoon (when Sally did not come and Elizabeth slept).

'Nowadays you never give a simple answer to anything.'

'There are no simple answers, are there. I used to think there were, before I started reading your books. But take jealousy, Othello was so jealous he killed his innocent wife. He didn't do it just because of Iago, because of evil rumour, but because he let the emotion get a hold on him, eat him up.'

'I must say I've never really understood *Othello*. I always thought it was a bit unlikely. He had only to ask her, to really ask her . . .'

'Well someone, and I think I can guess who, has told you Sally comes here for two hours. You sleep. Perhaps we make love again and again on the rug in front of the fire while the children play in the pen. We could do.'

'Do you?'

'No.'

Silence. Margot saw his point. She had to believe him, or not believe him and rationality had nothing to do with it. Ben took
160

up his glass and smiled at her, seeing her deep frown through the red wine.

'I think I am more Othello than you are. I am under the spell of a fixed idea which I cannot shake off. But it is nothing so reasonable as mere jealousy.'

He got up and started to pile dishes on the corner of the table.

'What idea?'

The Hamlet syndrome, he had read, is an outdated one. The law and religion and prisons have somehow put an end to man's need for personal revenge. And yet vigilante groups, and domestic murders, and terrorist reprisals, and . . . and Ben.

'Actually,' said Ben, moving the dishes into the kitchen, over his shoulder, 'times have changed since the Elizabethans, and you could ask Sally, because Sally, believe it or not, is more loyal to women than to men and if we had "dallied" she would have been the first to tell you.'

All in all life was becoming too complex for him and he longed for Margot to go back to work so that he could see what it was like living on his own with Elizabeth in the daytime. He also knew that he would have to alter her rhythm of sleeping and feeding and was a little apprehensive about his ability to do so, though Angela had declared him on one of her visits to be definitely the Father of the Moment (or had she said Flavour of the Month or something awful like that?) and Capable of Anything. She did this largely to annoy Andrew who took Ben upstairs after half an hour for a man to man talk during which Ben was unwilling to give him any advice but agreed to meet him at the sports club the very day Margot went back to work.

The office for the registration of births, deaths and marriages was situated, romantically enough, over a supermarket in the pedestrian precinct in town. Elizabeth was nearing six weeks old by the end of November and the legal deadline for registering her birth was drawing in. For some reason Ben was unwilling to enter their daughter on the Register of Existence. Was he subconsciously wanting to keep her a secret? Did he feel that once her birth was registered, she would one day have her death registered too, that she became official, and mortal? Margot, rediscovering the gifted, patient teacher in herself, reassured him that the act was only a formality and had no deeper significance.

'Quite a little family,' said Ben as they entered. He was in high spirits, Margot was pleased to note since she felt she had forced him to come, and been successful in allaying his fears of official-dom and bureaucracy, an understandable misgiving no doubt prevalent in the working classes.

'Well I don't feel like a family yet,' said Margot, 'just a couple with a baby. Maybe with two I would feel like a family.'

They sat and waited in an ante-chamber, surrounded by posters of far-off places, Singapore, Australia.

'Have we decided on Elizabeth then?' Margot had insisted on wearing her jeans and could hardly breathe now that Ben had winched her into them, lying flat on the bed.

'Yes, Elizabeth.'

They sat and waited for the registrar, Elizabeth in the sling on Benny's front, snuggling, slurping.

The registrar – a middle-aged woman determined to be Enlight-ened and Modern and Things – informed them that since they were not married they could choose whose surname the child would take. They had already discussed this and Margot had agreed she should take Ben's because, as he pointed out, then she would have less stigma of illegitimacy, should such a thing even exist when she would be old enough to notice. Enoch had Sally's name, and that was enough to persuade Margot that it was not a good idea, advertising the fact. Besides, she felt she owed him the honour, since he had once offered marriage to her, and was here under duress anyway.

So she was registered Elizabeth Ashe and since she was not to be christened – for even Margot's mother agreed this had no meaning other than a social one for the parents – it was the nearest she came to becoming a Statistically Real Person.

Afterwards, like a Real Family, they went to an American fast food restaurant just opened in the precinct and both had milk-shakes, Elizabeth sitting on Margot's knee at the stern of a make-believe boat, and Margot was full of wonder (and after the

162

milkshake, full of pain around her middle) at how far they had come since the birth, a mere six weeks ago.

In some ways she felt diminished, as if motherhood were already constraining her, but mostly she was grateful for the addition of Elizabeth into her life.

It was true, though, that her outlook had narrowed since the birth. She felt less cocksure about life, felt that she was neither fully mother nor fully worker any more and sometimes short bursts of worry about the baby (along the lines of cot death and so on) would take hold and send unfamiliar spasms of panic through her system. She was no longer the same person, if only because she now felt more dependent on Ben than she had ever done.

30 *Diary 3*

Baby was born on the night of the thirteenth of October at 6.43 and weighed exactly eight pounds.

I feel as if I have finally joined the Human Race: birth, death – the ultimate once-only experiences.

Due to shortness of time I can only now make weekly entries.

Week 1
Regained birthweight. Feeding 4-hourly. Sleeps. Always pushing feet out of covering. Mother came to visit; stayed with Ben. He wonderful with her. And with E. and cheers me up.

In great pain and much drugged. Think I shouted something horrible to B. or Mum – can't remember what, though.

Week 2
At home: feeding randomly. Ben walks her to sleep by 2 a.m. He also baths her (I'm too sore). Then we lay her nude in front of the fire to kick. She is too sleepy in the daytime to feed. Ben won't let me go to her in the night – says I need my sleep, so some bottle then I guess. Ben is wonderful with her. Better than me for quieting her.

Week 3
On bottle now completely. Midwife pleased with weight gain

163

and she followed keys held in front of her with eyes! Loves her mobiles, also being in bed with us after her bath. Took her to shops in pram.

Week 4
Breasts sore. Mastitis – Ben used electric shaver to vibrate plus antibiotics. Midwife warned me – my milk curdling! I missed Fireworks Night.

Week 5
Cleared garden so she could sit in pram. She smiles at us now, whenever she sees a face. Any face to be honest. Worried about vomiting but B. says it is only 'possetting' and natural. Thank God someone has read the books. She found her thumb.

Almost had row with Ben over Sally's visiting while I nap but he won't argue – he cites literary examples of things!

Week 6
Ben finally agreed to go and we registered her as Elizabeth Ashe. Afterwards had milkshakes and wandered about shops like ordinary people. Seems everyone in Sheffield has a Babypak on their front or back. We smile at each other like bus drivers passing on a wet day flash their lights at each other. Or the Masonic Handshake.

Week 7
1st December
Chest and head off mat when on tummy; 'talking' in phrases; so almost words now. Ben showed me some of the booty Mother bought when she was here (ridiculous stuff some of it) and we laughed. He asked me what a Yuppie was. Explained humorously about material ambitions, smart cars, clothes, professional aspirations, waxed coats and Turkish holidays, etc. Oh, then you are one I guess, he said. The nerve! Certainly not, I said. Then should we add to the definition, he asked, the additional point that a Yuppie would be offended by being so described. Or words to that effect. No, I said, I insist I cannot be a Yuppie. Why not, then? He made me say it (he does this now, never leaves anything alone until I've *said* it – as if there is one Big Thing that

he is wanting me to say, which I never do) 'because of you'. He wasn't as upset as I thought. I see, was all he said, I see.

Week 9
15th December
Since she now weighs 13lbs 3oz, gave first Farex. Loved it. Seems older and more independent and aggressive, but in a nice way.

I have asked Ben for a leather-bound page-at-a-view diary for Christmas. Have bought him a glossy childcare book published in Australia, of all places. Must say, I never would have believed, this time last year, that I would be buying him a *book* for Christmas.

What am I saying?

Or anything at all.

Whatever did we do to pass the time before Elizabeth?

Week 10
22nd December
Travelled to Bournemouth to spend Christmas with Mother. Packing the car up was a major event – in the end I left it to him and played with E. The amount of equipment needed for one small person was astonishing. Ben had even bought four dozen disposable nappies – well, twelve a day, he says. He also dismantled the cot and the high chair, putting the bolts into separate labelled envelopes. Her bath, her changing mat, her toys, and finally – the pram itself, off its wheels, folded somehow and the chassis somewhere else.

'Glad we disposed of the sports car,' he said, when he had finished.

'At this rate Christmas will be over by the time we get there.' If waiting for him to complete the packing was Purgatory, the journey was Hell. For a start I stupidly thought E. would fall asleep somewhere south of Chesterfield. She never slept at all. She wasn't actually sick until Winchester, but then spectacularly so. And to add to the horror, I was sick trying to clear it up. Isn't family life wonderful, Ben kept saying, driving on as if nothing were wrong.

Oh God, Bournemouth out of season – I had forgotten. Young people hang about the skating-rink with the sides of their heads shaved to look dangerous, one motor cycle between eight boys.

165

And the Lower Pleasure Gardens, full all summer with mini-golfers and bright annuals, now a wasteland of empty beds and closed down hot-dog stands. Along the beaches which annually contain a thousand grilling people per foot, now just a long curved stretch in which tweedy people walk their dogs three times a day, their headscarves flapping in the chill winds which the local people believe come off the Russian steppes.

Mother delighted to see us, though late by four hours, but she seemed more thrilled to see Elizabeth and Ben than to see me. All traces of 'He's here,' etc. gone, thank God.

Christmas Day itself was wonderful. Mother had bought about twenty new toys for E., a large bottle of whisky for Ben and a book token, which is what she has given me for the last ten years. Ben gave me *the* perfect diary – he hadn't forgotten. He and Mum seem real pals and he helped her with the cooking and over Christmas dinner related a most unlikely story about what he had done last Christmas – including a death-defying climb over a snowy roof to retrieve an aerial and a visit to a nuclear bunker. So Mother *knows* he is not an unemployed philosopher.

Ben and Mother had too much to drink and Ben tried to teach her to Cha Cha Cha to some old music they found. Apparently Mother knew what he meant when he said 'now for the New Yorker' and things like that.

Week 12

HURRAY! I want this to be the first word in my new diary. Everything is wonderful except that on the 6th January I shall have to return to work.

Feeding pattern finally established, so she has five bottle feeds and one 'meal' in evening, and no night-time waking (so far as I know).

Transferred her to a cot. Lying on her back in here she can now see and watches with fascination her own hands. If something is handy within the range of her swipe, she pulls it towards her, e.g., Ben's crocheted blanket of a million colours which she seems to call 'Mudmud'. We have to be careful changing her nappy now because she will grab that too if she can, presumably mistaking it for a white Mudmud.

Enjoys making a loud scream for fun. Scares the life out of me,

166

but Ben encourages her. 'Let it all out,' he says, and she does it again.

The beginnings of imitation now?

31 *The First Bomb*

Fortunately Dorothea had been unable to sell her house during the Christmas holidays even though she had dedicated herself to it, even cancelling her annual New Year Party, and so was able to lend her valuable assistance and advice to Sheffield High School for another term. This also lifted from the shoulders of the Headmaster the heavy burden of finding someone to replace so dedicated and talented a worker.

Or at least to postpone an appointment for a term. With any luck he would not need to appoint anyone until next September.

Did Margot really think, Dorothea asked her, that now that she has all the responsibilities of motherhood, and single parent motherhood at that, that she would be eligible for a Scale 4 post as head of department? She was only Scale 2 now, though admittedly that was largely because the geography department had 'stolen' scale points which the English department deserved.

Margot was devastated by this analysis of her career prospects, and almost argued with Dorothea, pointing out that she too had the responsibilities of motherhood, that she too had gone from Scale 2 to 4, that it was sexism to be prejudiced against her because she was a single parent.

No one is prejudiced, replied Dorothea, on the contrary. Here we employ black, gay, Muslim teachers without reference to their religious or racial background. But circumstances have to dictate *promotions*. The Head must appoint the person who can best carry out the duties of a head of department.

'And he will ask your advice,' said Margot, trying to sound friendly.

'He must advertise the post – that is the law,' said Dorothea.

'But he need not appoint from outside.'

'He can only appoint someone he has interviewed.'

The bomb fell. It fell on Margot.

'Will he not interview me then?'

'No, I think not. It would not be kind, I told him, to raise your hopes by interviewing you only to dash them again when you were turned down. I have tried to protect you from that kind of disappointment. It is the very last thing you need at this time in your life. After all, Margot, dear, I am very fond of you. Of you both. You must come to dinner some time, before the house is sold. Iseult would love to baby-sit for you.'

Margot phoned home at lunchtime but got no answer. Perhaps he was taking Elizabeth out for a walk in the pram. On his own, or with . . . No, don't start thinking things. Oh, God, J. came by and enquired after the baby. He was now a full-time paid member of staff and found it was much less like hard work than being a student.

Margot told him how the bottom of her world had just been blown away in a puff of St Moritz. He put an arm around her shoulder and led her out of the building towards the car-park. This innocent gesture of comfort was interpreted by those fifth formers lurking by the entrance to the sports hall as proof positive that the rumour that J. was the father was *true*.

They went out in his car (an old mini) to the pub for a sandwich and a drink and Margot felt almost merry when they returned.
'I expect you'll miss what's-her-name, the gym mistress.'
'Gym mistress?'
'Angela was it?'
'Oh, her.' She had never thought of Angela as a gym mistress. 'No, just my job prospects.'
J. advised her to make it clear she was applying for jobs in other counties, to call their bluff. That's what he'd do. Yes, but then you haven't got a house and a child and so on.
Technicalities, he said.

'You're a devil with a squash racquet.'
'I'm a devil anyway, even without one,' replied Benny. They drifted painfully over to the bar and Andrew ordered two beers.
'Angela tells me all men are devils underneath.'
'Underneath what?'
They laughed, lasciviously.

*

168

Underneath the sign 'Crèche' on the door at the left of the squash courts, a glass window allowing one-way vision only, was a printed sign which read

MOTHERS WHO ARE MEMBERS OR GUESTS

MAY LEAVE CHILDREN HERE

FOR ONE HOUR

Ben, after three beers with Andrew, borrowed a pen from him and crossed out MOTHERS, writing PARENTS above it.

'That's a blow for Women's Lib,' said Andrew, leaning against the doorframe.

'I don't see what Women's Lib has to do with it,' said Ben, opening the door into the crèche. Elizabeth saw him, from a bouncing cradle on the other side of the room, and smiled.

They sat for lunch, the three of them, by a window overlooking a stretch of grass which could not decide whether it was a cricket pitch or a tennis-court and was meantime being used by the local canine population as a toilet.

Andrew insisted on treating Ben and on knowing that the waiter's name was Richard. Even though the waiter was called George, Andrew knew, deep down, and didn't mind telling Ben, that it was really Richard.

George, who was really Richard, suddenly noticed that Ben's rucksack contained a baby and asked them to move out into the Family Room. This incensed Andrew, himself a 'father of a small baby, though a boy' and a row started to happen. Ben dragged Andrew out into the veranda and ordered some sandwiches.

'But it is ten below out here,' said Andrew.

'Little Bet and I like fresh air. And it might help you sober up,' said Ben, wishing Margot hadn't got the car today. But he was fully prepared to walk all the way home, dog-shit or no dog-shit, rather than expose Little Bet to the risk of drunken driving.

When he had eaten, sobered, apologised to George and signed the chit, Andrew asked Ben what he was doing about getting a job.

'But I have a job, looking after Elizabeth.'

'I mean a real job. You can't go on like this, can you?'

They walked down to the car-park, Ben deep in thought.

'I might start a business, repairing televisions.'

'Ah, but you need a bit of capital for that,' said Andrew as if he had just discovered a Great Truth.

'Yes, you're right there, Andrew. Shall I drive?'

32 *Telecommunications*

Elizabeth was finally asleep that Sunday afternoon and Margot celebrated a whole week back at work by putting Joni Mitchell on the turntable, loud, and flopping on the sofa in the sitting-room.

She let the sound wash over her.

Ben walked in from the hall and turned it down.

'I'm phoning Sharon now, I need a bit of hush.'

'Oh, leave it, please, just for a few minutes.'

'Doesn't that interminable droning get on your nerves?'

'What? Where did you learn such long words, darling?'

'From you, darling. Now keep quiet, will you?'

He went to phone. He always phones Sharon Sundays. Margot doesn't know what it means to have a sister but this transcontinental phoning seems excessive to her. One Sunday he phones her, the next she him. Why do they bother? What do they say to each other? She is not jealous, not exactly – how could you be jealous of a sister? – but this excessive phoning. Why did she think it would stop once she was back at work?

Silence but for the muttering of Ben on the phone in the hall. She strains to hear. Nothing sensible can she make out. He comes back into the room and puts the record back on, loud.

'Oh, don't.'

'One minute you . . .'

'It's okay, just leave it. How was Sharon?'

'Fine.' He turns his back on her and walks into the kitchen.

She is always just fine. His women – mother, sister, daughter. These are the important women in his life, the blood-relations, not *her*. She is just a stepping-stone between his mother and his

170

daughter, nobody. She felt the need for a fight welling up inside her. Nothing clears the air like a fight.

'Ben, why don't I matter to you?' He was taking nappies out of the washing-machine in the kitchen and draping them in exact patterns over something he called The Clowsorse, to be put before the fire to fug up the room with a not unpleasant smelling steam.

'You do matter.' He didn't look up.

'But why am I not the most important woman in your life? I ought to be.'

Now he looked up at her, his face blank.

'But you are. You are the Prime Mover of the Universe.' He often said cryptic clever things like this now, as if he had been engaged on some research into their lives rather than a little light reading. 'Everything is because of you,' he added.

Margot couldn't bear to say, then why don't you talk to me, engage with me. It was such a cliché, such a ridiculously stupid situation to have got into, the sort of thing she feared so much would happen if she lived with Andrew that she had thrown up the chance.

Little Elizabeth cried out from upstairs, the Kiddy Alert transmitting it to them.

'I'll go,' said Margot and shot out of the room.

Elizabeth was crying. Margot had meant to scoop her up and comfort her, she had even anticipated the wet, smooth, petal-warm cheek against hers juddering and then going still, but instead when she got to the cot she found herself leaning over it and adding to the weeping herself with hot, fat tears which fell like drips of blood onto the silk edge of her blanket. Elizabeth wailed louder, or it seemed louder.

'Oh, please shut up,' she said to the baby.

Ben was behind her. He bent down beside her and gently lifted the baby. She stopped crying immediately. *Immediately*. It's not fair; he has only to think of her and she smiles.

'Daddy's here. Daddy's here,' he crooned, taking her over to the window. He opened the rainbow blind with one hand, showing her the world, the grey autumn afternoon twilight, almost winter.

171

'Why don't you go and lie down,' he said to Margot without turning round, 'you seem tired. It's been a long week.'

'I am not tired,' said Margot, like the spoilt child who stamps her foot – I am not cross, I AM NOT!

But she lay down on their bed, to prove something to him. See I am lying down and not sleeping. He came in without the baby a few minutes later. Damn, how he calms her down so easily! He stood in the doorway in the shape of an 'S', braced against its sides.

'You angry because I phoned my sister?' he asked.

'No, of course not.'

'What's the matter then?'

Margot started to weep and buried her head in her pillows and said something Ben could not hear. He waited.

'Say it out loud, will you?'

'She is not really mine at all!'

Ben laughed and approached the bed, where he sat, but without touching her.

'Well I didn't find her in the cabbage patch.' She turned round. 'How can you feel close to her when you are not here? By magic? You have got to try harder, like a man who goes out to work all day. If you want her love you have got to earn it. It's no good waiting till she's old enough to read and then writing her a letter all about genetic coding.'

'How can I then when I am out all day?'

'Next weekend, when you are less tired, take her out on your own. Visit someone. Just the two of you.'

'Who? I don't know anyone.'

Ben, wearied of her suddenly, started out of the bedroom. 'Well, if you want to wallow there in self-pity, you do so, I've got ironing to do.'

'You're so lucky. Andrew does bloody nothing and less than that if he can manage. Oh I knew when I took him on he wasn't going to be the world's best cook and bottlewasher. After all the kitchen was just a shell really; he ate out every night. Even the Hoover was a mystery to him: he used to have a woman come in to clean. We won't need her now, will we, he says. But shit, I need some help. He *has* to stay for a drink with his colleagues,

172

he says. Business is business. Half an hour a day he sees Jasper. He knows his secretary better. And then, to add insult to injury, never mind if I have a period, cystitis, and a migraine headache, he's got to have his leg over at least three times a week. I could do without it, Margot, all of it, I really could. It's not as if he has the first idea, as you know yourself.'

'He has the first idea but not the *second* as I recall.'

'I dream about netball with the lower third, and trampolining with the sixth form girls – going to work, leaving all this and just getting out of it. Getting the hell out.'

They were sitting in Angela's back room, adjacent to the kitchen. The two babies were lying face down on a rug surrounded by bright plastic things and sticky pools and cloths. Margot was 'having Elizabeth all to herself' for the Saturday afternoon of her second week back at work, and had chosen to visit Angela for the first time in her house, with Elizabeth. Andrew was out, fortunately. Or perhaps unfortunately, for it gave Angela the opportunity to thus rail against him which Margot thought, under the circumstances, both unfair and in bad taste. After all, no one asked her to steal him away, did they?

Angela's house was 'the proverbial tip' as she would have put it. Margot had never seen such mess. Angela had streaks of old mascara under her eyes, her hair was unbrushed and she had not lost the weight yet. Also she was smoking again. Margot got up to open a window behind her, for the sake of the babies more than herself.

'But I thought this was what you wanted most of all.'

'Oh yes, what a fool I was.'

Margot sighed. It all seemed so unnecessary. Why couldn't she just clear up the place, smarten herself up and get on with it?

'I have heard every programme on Radio Four from seven in the morning to nine at night for the last three months. I can recite the shipping forecast order for you.'

Margot laughed. 'You haven't been wasting your time then, I see.'

'I've even thought of getting a nanny and going back to work. But you can't get good nannies here. If they're any good they go

173

to London where the big money is to join the new Servant Class.
And the stories you hear!'
  'What?'

Angela told Margot what she had heard at the clinic, at the
Mother and Baby club attached to the local playgroup, at the
shops, and from the health visitor.

Margot couldn't help remembering the stories girls told each
other in the changing-rooms after hockey or netball, of baby-
sitters phoning the parents to ask when the turkey would be
cooked only to be told there was no turkey. Then what have I
been basting these last three hours? And so she agreed with
Angela that you have got to be safe from such horrors, to protect
yourself from tragedy like that.

Changing the subject to dispel her own nightmare imaginings,
Margot was able to tell Angela all the new gossip from school,
but she didn't seem to be at all interested.

Of course it all served her right, for having such a brilliant time
producing the baby, and it was with a certain pleasure that
Margot told Ben that night what chaos Angela and Andrew lived
in and how she gave the marriage a year at the most.

He only listened with half an ear, applying a second coat of
disinfectant to the kitchen floor. Now that Elizabeth was almost
crawling he paid particular attention to the floors, and was able
to spot a sharp object nestling evilly in thick pile carpet such as
they had in the sitting-room from eight yards away.

  'Andrew told me they're thinking of having another one soon,'
was all he said.

  'Do you want another one soon?' she asked, suddenly ame-
nable to anything this dear, useful man should want.

  'Definitely not. One is quite enough, don't you think?'

  'Absolutely.'

And he was so undemanding. In fact it was she who made that
eighteen-inch journey across the sahara of the silk sheets that
night and so exhausted him that he was almost irritable when
Elizabeth woke an hour later. Gradually he was putting a stop to
their nocturnal habits, his with Elizabeth that is, but it was taking

174

time. Nowadays he had only three hours solid sleep at nights, the rest he took in snatches in the early morning, with the baby dozing on his bare chest, and in the afternoon when she slept, with her in the double bed. But he didn't feel Margot would understand if he said he was too tired.

33 *Diary 4*

Saturday 30th January
Visited Angela again today with E. Jasper crawling already! House in mess still, etc.

Had to leave sooner than I meant to because I had forgotten to bring Mudmud – how could I? Before I left I gave her a few pointers about being organised, etc. She really must get herself together. She didn't take the advice in quite the spirit I meant it.

Showed her again to Mrs Harrison in more detail, who commented – strong muscles, pretty, delicate face and very alert. Mrs H. ought to know – mother of six apparently!

Don't think I shall have her to myself every Saturday – it's so exhausting without Ben.

In fact, no sooner had I returned and located Mudmud than Ben said he was going out, just as I was going to ask him for a cup of tea.

On his way out he reminded me it was time to start preparing dinner. Dinner!

The problem is that I failed to think ahead here, *re* the freezer, and what to do with Elizabeth while cooking. She would *not* sit quietly in highchair for me, so had to carry her about, hunting for tins of baked beans, trying to work out Ben's system, if there is any, of food storage.

Utterly defeated, beans burnt, Ben came home sniffing imaginary dinner in the air.

Do I detect the smell of burnt something, he asked. I nearly threw something at him but all that was to hand was Elizabeth. Explained my problems and admitted he must be a magician to make a meal for us all every night.

Ah, then these fish and chips won't go to waste, he said, bringing a packet out from under his jacket. Never enjoyed a meal more.

175

Think I am not what they call a 'born mother'. However the intensity of my love for her is deepening – she is the centre of everything.

Sunday 31st January
Suddenly she wants that doll Mrs Harrison gave her which I have rashly named Pollyanna. I spoil her – I want her to have everything since she can't have me all the time.

Tuesday 2nd February
Ben took her for her Diphtheria, Polio, Whooping Cough and Tetanus immunisation, without telling me about it. Just as well, I would have been worried sick and unable to concentrate at work. However, no adverse reactions it seems. I kept feeling her damp little forehead all evening for signs of fever. Asleep she is perfection made flesh.

Wednesday 3rd February
Sudden progress when I got home: she can roll over on her own. Any minute now she will be crawling! And she is only four months. Wow! I'm sure Jasper was still on his back at this age – she must be very bright.

Thursday 4th February
Elizabeth was exactly four months or 16 weeks old today and Ben insisted on us having a celebration. One candle for each month on a carob cake.

Ben had made the cake which contained all whole ingredients, no sugar and no real chocolate. He had decorated it with yoghurt and crushed nuts. Elizabeth was very excited when we lit the candles and sang to her and nearly fell out of the high chair with chortling.

When we'd got her to bed B. asked me if I was happy. I said I could not imagine being happier in my entire life and he said that was all that mattered. ** 10/10 no doubt about it. I have just snuck downstairs to have a cup of tea (sheer bliss must be keeping me awake) and thought I'd write this tonight. Does anyone deserve such happiness?

34 *Nuked!*

No (sorry).

On Friday the fifth of February Margot pulled up by the front steps, nodded to Mrs Harrison cleaning her steps and let herself in. Mrs Harrison was trying to start an urgent conversation, no doubt about the new Pakis moved in next door, but Margot pretended not to hear and went straight in.

'Ben, I'm home.'

No answer. The pushchair was missing from its station by the front door. They must be out later than usual. Perhaps she didn't nap and he's taken her out to lull her to sleep.

She shut the door and hung up her coat, made herself some tea and sat with her feet up and the radio on, in the front room, relaxed, waiting.

She was still waiting at seven o'clock, though now somewhat anxiously. He must be visiting. Perhaps he has friends she knows nothing about. It had also crossed her mind that they had had an accident, Elizabeth was in hospital, dead, both dead, but these thoughts passed rapidly out of her mind when she remembered how careful he always was. He wouldn't even risk crossing the road with Elizabeth unless there was *no* traffic in sight or sound.

At nine o'clock she began to search the house, though there was no rational reason for doing so. Something was missing from every room, and with each room she entered, her panic increased.

From the kitchen, bottles, formula, spoutmugs and bibs were missing, from their bedroom the majority of Ben's belongings, clothes, electric razor. From Elizabeth's room just about *everything*. Now she screamed out loud. He had left her, and taken the baby with him.

Had they argued that morning? She searched her brain. The previous night? No, on the contrary, they had . . . When? What?

Why? Why? Why? It must be one of his weird jokes, a test of some sort.

She ran along the corridor and downstairs and to the door of his mother's old room, the room she had never entered, and pushed open the door. The room was almost empty and inches thick in dust.

In one corner was a television set she had never seen before and beside it on the floor a video recorder. A note lay on top of the video which simply said 'Press Operate and then Play'. It was the first time she had ever seen his handwriting.

First the screen was full of white dots and hissed at her. Then it cleared and Ben appeared, smiling idiotically like people about to have their photographs taken.

The image of Ben spoke:

So you have finally come into my mother's room. You never came when Mrs Elizabeth Ashe was alive. That's a shame. But that's in the past.

Little Elizabeth and I will be half-way to Australia by the time you see this. Sharon and her family are expecting us. This house is half yours. My half I have sold – to Andrew Furnace. He has bought it as an investment and will be moving a tenant into the flat upstairs.

Margot – you have been very stupid. I just have to say this. Even Heathcliff got custody of little Cathy in the end. Since you won't be seeing her again, I have filmed her for you, on the changing mat.

There followed two excruciating minutes of Elizabeth in action, smiling into the camera. Ben had overdubbed this section.

I hope you understand this, Margot. By the way – thank you for the ten out of ten. Goodbye.

Then the form of Elizabeth and the voice of Ben disappeared into the hissing dots again.

Now Margot knew why, she knew why as soon as she heard the words Mrs Elizabeth Ashe, for no one had thought to tell her that her daughter was named after Ben's mother. Until that point a small part of her still thought this must be some awful practical joke. But then she had often felt that she was merely a stepping-stone between his mother and his daughter, but until now she had not realised quite how literally. It had occurred to

178

her once just fleetingly, before she knew him, that he might have blamed her for his mother's death, but it was an idea so preposterous, she thought, that she had banished it from her mind as any sane person would.

So in full possession of her faculties and most of the facts at last, Margot fell down and wept for herself and for her lost baby and wanted only to die that very instant. She fell where Benny had fallen in the first wave of his belated grief and the first flush of his fatherhood.

Then she staggered out into the hall and picked up the phone and wept into it, knowing only Sharon's maiden name and the fact that she lived in Perth was so obviously not enough.

Then for a moment her mind cleared and she thought she could apply to the Law. After all this was kidnap. Yes, and Andrew was a lawyer. But Andrew had colluded in this – he must have known Ben's plans. And Angela! Oh, now her heart sank. Doubly destroyed – for not only did this mean that Ben had taken advice from Andrew, but she realised that she could not have Elizabeth back in any case without Ben. She was more his than hers. She could not look after her without him. She would have to employ someone. What court would even look favourably on that. Let alone her heart. She was going to have to accept it. *Accept* it – how could she?

So, not only has Margot lost her baby, but she has lost the illusion of being loved, for he must have planned this all along, even in those intimate moments, even when . . . and that hurts almost more than the realisation of the quintessential perfection of his revenge.

Margot, English mistress now thinking fast like the hundreds of pupils she had put under examination stress, finally sees the plot: there was nothing he could deprive her of which really mattered, so he gave it to her and then took it away. Oh how clever, oh what a demi-devil after all!

179

35 *Fallout*

Margot killed Ben's mother. Did you forget that? Ben didn't. It is not simply a question of revenge, for Ben might have run amok and killed Margot or her mother, spending the rest of his life at Her Majesty's Pleasure.

You thought Ben would do something more subtle, being now so well self-educated, so almost *middle class* – God forbid? Or that, if he had planned this he would waver, being overwhelmed by his love for his daughter? No, the truth is, nothing ever overwhelmed him so much as the untimely death of his mother, who was only sixty-four when she died.

Also he might have grown to love Margot, as I did (alas); but in fact she always blew it, being only human. He gave her chances to discover and disarm him (you couldn't have missed them, they were so obvious to everyone but her), but she was unable to take those chances. Margot could not live her life on the off-chance, she *had* to be safe.

So, Ben's plan, his tank, if you remember, has served him well. He has had to modify it but little since that first night when he and the world were first bereft of Bet Senior.

Do not worry about Bet Junior: Ben knows she is a person in her own right, though the resemblance is more than striking. For he has lifted the lid of the tank, climbed out with the Babypak on and Little Bet (and Mudmud and Pollyanna) fast asleep centimetres from her favourite person's rapid heartbeats, and has hailed a passing aeroplane. In other words, he has not taken the tank with him to Australia.

Where Sharon and Ron and the boys are expecting them, and are a little relieved, though sorry of course, to hear that Ben's girlfriend passed away during the difficult birth. These things happen though, and Sharon always wanted a girl to look after, not that she will ever have the chance for more than an hour or

180

two. Which is hard on her because she has been waiting patiently for four months for them to come.

Not to worry at all, since Ben is no psychopath: after all he has not hurt a living person, not bodily, not legally (only that healed-over gash of Margot's worries him sometimes, but less and less with the passing years). There is nothing imprisonable he has done. Margot is the one who will be in prison, for the rest of her life.

Always one way or another. Even a child lost in the last stages of a pregnancy, or the earlier, is a gap, a hiatus, a tragedy. No woman ever forgets the loss, or recovers wholly. Margot will certainly never recover from her loss, from all her losses.

Margot decides, wandering round the ground floor looking for her wicker chair, that she will tell everyone that Ben has taken the baby to visit his relatives in Australia and will be back one day. Then she will only gradually have to deal with their theories.
For they will all have theories about this. Margot's mother will see the whole episode as an opportunity for them both to serve Christ; Andrew will tell her that he warned her not to trust him, and was himself hoodwinked into buying half the property so that Ben could start a small business of his own with the capital; Angela will blame her for not marrying him, not legalising her position; Sally will say she should have been suspicious when he prevented her from breastfeeding – he always wanted absolute power over the child; Dorothea says her judgement about people leaves something to be desired and under the circumstances it is just as well she is not in the running for the headship; J. says it is just damned bad luck and would she like to come to Senegal on holiday with him; but Mrs Harrison, for once, gets it completely right and tells the regulars at the Co-op that Benedict Ashe has wreaked a dastardly but in some ways admirable revenge for the death of his mother. But nobody believes a word of it: it is far too improbable.

Margot takes the wicker chair from her bedroom, the one where she had sat and failed to feed Elizabeth, and drags it up to the empty flat. She sits there, by the french window to the balcony,

181

looking out over the lime trees and Sheffield beyond, where she once felt so safe.

And she is still sitting there when Sally and Baby Enoch arrive to take up their tenancy.